STABBED IN THE SOLARIUM

A MOORECLIFF MANOR CAT COZY MYSTERY BOOK 2

LEIGHANN DOBBS

CHAPTER ONE

*S*ometime *after midnight:*

The solarium was kind of creepy at night. The plants of all shapes and sizes were mere shadows in the dark, lurking in every corner of the large room. The air was heavy with humidity and the scent of moist earth. A cricket had gotten inside, and he chirped mechanically in the corner.

Vines had grown up along the tall arched windows that made up three of the walls. There were so many vines and plants that one could hardly even see outside. Still, a sliver of moonlight had managed to filter in, and Shirley could see the stars through the tops of the ten-foot-tall windows.

It was an odd place to meet. Shirley took a sip of her margarita for liquid courage. Not that she needed courage; she was used to clandestine meetings.

The door creaked open, and Shirley swung around, sloshing the margarita over the rim of her glass. "Ha! So you came!"

The figure stayed in the shadows, giving Shirley pause. Was it the person she had been expecting or someone else? Why didn't they say something?

She leaned forward and squinted, trying to make out who it was. "Did you bring the money?"

The person didn't answer. Shirley took another sip of her drink. It didn't really matter who it was. Any money was good money, and she'd discovered most would pay plenty of it to keep their secrets. And Shirley knew a lot of secrets.

"Why are you lurking in the shadows? No one can see in here. The windows are covered with vines and leaves." Shirley gestured around the room, sloshing more of her drink. "Just give me the money, and let's get this over with."

The person stepped forward, and Shirley could see who it was. "Oh! It's you. You sent me the note?"

"Yes, it was me."

"Okay, well get on with it, then."

The person lifted their arm, and Shirley

wondered for a split second if they were going to go on a long tirade. She hoped not—she wasn't really up for it, and she should be getting to bed. But then she saw the moonlight glinting off the blade of the knife.

Too late, she tried to dodge the blade arcing down toward her chest. The margarita glass slipped out of her hand and smashed to the floor. Shirley quickly followed it. The last thing she heard was the solarium door banging shut as her killer fled out into the woods.

CHAPTER TWO

The next morning…

Moorecliff Manor was a hive of activity, filled with out-of-town guests, waitstaff, and friends who had all come to attend the memorial celebration for Archibald Moorecliff. Archie's funeral had been a small affair for close family only, and his widow, Daisy, had spent weeks planning the celebration so the rest of the large Moorecliff family and out-of-town friends could pay their respects.

Araminta Moorecliff, Archie's octogenarian aunt, had dressed in her finest neon-pink outfit especially for the occasion. She'd even topped it off with a bright-pink wide-brimmed sun hat and added a lime-green sash, which she had tied around her neck, to finish the perfect celebratory ensemble most suited for the day's outing: the reveal of a new memorial garden Daisy had had created in honor of her late husband.

At the moment, however, Araminta was seated at one of the small round tables the staff had set up in the dining room to help accommodate the large number of guests staying at Moorecliff Manor, enjoying a light breakfast with a handful of others from the Moorecliff family.

Arun and Sasha, her Siamese cats, were winding their way around the room, slinking under tables and skulking against walls. They were smart enough to seek only the attention of those in the Moorecliff clan who actually liked cats, accepting a gentle petting here and a morsel of food there. Their intelligent blue eyes scanned the room for their next victim as they darted from table to table.

Daisy, who was dressed impeccably in an off-white linen designer suit, her ebony hair tucked back in a chignon at the base of her neck, sat at the head of the main table. Her stepdaughter, Stephanie, was seated at her right. Steph had had a hard time accepting Daisy as a stepmother, and Araminta hoped this could be a time of healing for both of them. She truly wished that her grandniece would come to see that Daisy really had married her father for love and not for his money, as many in the family had assumed, and that she would come to think of Daisy as family.

Poor Stephanie did look a little under the weather, the dark circles under her hazel eyes giving away the strain of the past few weeks. Araminta saw a rare smile on Stephanie's face as she bent to pet the cats, her hand gliding over the silvery fur on Arun's back and giving a few scratches between his mink-brown ears. She hoped the girl had found her own sense of closure these past weeks since her father's unexpected death. She'd spent almost every waking hour in the gardens with Yancy, helping him —and the crew of locals he'd called in to help with the undertaking—to create a special corner of the grounds that would remind future generations of Moorecliffs of Archibald's existence.

Poor Reginald, Archie's son. He hadn't been as involved in the creation of the garden to honor his father's memory as his sister had, and he would not be taking part in today's unveiling, but he was taking a step in the right direction. Out of gratitude for his stepmother's help with saving him from the harsh repercussions of doing business with Tony "the Fist" Romano, Reggie was attending a special three-day seminar for Gamblers Anonymous and would not be home until the day after the memorial's unveiling. The timing was unfortunate but couldn't have been avoided.

Despite the seriousness of the matter, the scamp was likely thrilled to have escaped having to deal with the Moorecliff family en masse. A few members at a time, he could handle, but when the aunts and cousins from several generations descended upon the manor at one time, he'd always found a convenient excuse to make himself scarce. Looking around at the motley crew, Araminta couldn't much blame him.

Today, however, Araminta knew he would have preferred to be in attendance. He missed his father a great deal, though he dealt with his own grief in a way quite different from his sister. While Stephanie had thrown herself into helping create the memorial garden, Reggie had thrown himself into learning as much as he could about the day-to-day workings of the family business.

Araminta was proud of her great-nephew for applying himself. He would become a valuable asset to the business in the future. For the moment, however, her late nephew had left everything in the capable hands of his father's widow.

"I knew she was a gold digger from the moment I met her!" someone at the table next to Araminta's whispered. There was a sting of envy edging the woman's tone. Araminta almost turned to correct the woman, because she knew Daisy better than any of them. But then there was more…

"She's not even a Moorecliff! What was Archibald thinking to leave her in charge of the entire company?"

Araminta heard a low chuckle, and then, "Don't worry. Shirley said she'll fix her, good and proper. She knows something about her past. Something truly horrid. And she knows the truth about Reginald. You've all noticed he isn't here, but Shirley says it's not because he got stuck in the Himalayas with his skiing buddies, like we've been told."

"Wait—Shirley has dirt on Daisy? Ooh!"

"Shirley has dirt on everyone. She even told me she knew Bernard was embezzling from Moorecliff Motors for years!"

Bernard Moorecliff was the reason a special memorial was needed to begin with. For years, he'd controlled operations of the West Coast division of Moorecliff Motors, while Archie was CEO of the entire company and took care of things on the East Coast. But he'd gotten greedy and wanted everything to himself. So he'd poisoned his brother and landed himself in prison for the murder—but not before Daisy discovered he was also stealing from the company. The courts had added another crime to his lifelong sentence: embezzlement.

"Where is Shirley, anyway? I could have sworn she said she'd be here early this morning."

One of the guests snorted into her orange juice. "Probably sleeping it off in her room upstairs. She was drunk last night. Too drunk, if you ask me. She was trying to hold court but losing ground and started threatening to spill all the family secrets."

"Do you think there are more? After embezzlement and murder, you'd think there wouldn't be much to top those," someone said.

"I'll bet she's with that gardener guy. They had a fling years ago, you know. She had it bad, our Shirley. I heard she used to sneak the poor fellow upstairs in the dumbwaiter!"

A round of giggles followed the revelation.

"Maybe we should look for her in there? Shirley was so drunk last night, she may have passed out on the way down to retrieve her lover."

"Oh, but Shirley isn't the only one who went a little crazy for the Moorecliff gardener," another whisperer chimed in. "I hear Charlotte, Betty, and Anastasia had a thing for him too…"

Araminta was about to step in, to stop their gossip before things got out of hand, when the cats caught her eye. They were over by the window, looking out as if they'd seen something. Wait, they had! Someone was lurking around outside the windows. After the conversation she'd just heard, she wondered if it was Yancy helping Shirley sneak back to her room before anyone decided to join them outside. Or maybe they'd decided to have another go this morning?

Whichever may have been the case, Araminta decided she did not want to see whatever the two of them might be up to. Instead, she turned her attention back to her breakfast, but she made a mental note to caution Yancy. In this family, it paid to be discreet when one decided to… do whatever they were doing together.

A short while later, Daisy signaled an end to breakfast. It was time for everyone to head out to the gardens!

Araminta headed out with the rest of the crowd, but then something else drew her eye.

Oh, no. This could not be a good sign.

Sasha and Arun had raced ahead to the solarium, then they drew up quite suddenly. After a few turns back and forth with their tails straight up in the air, Araminta became worried. She knew their actions meant they'd found something that begged her attention. The last time they'd acted that way, there had been a murder. But that couldn't be the reason now. What were the odds of that happening at Moorecliff Manor again in such a short period of time?

Breaking away from the rest of the crowd, she hurried toward the solarium. She would just have a quick peek inside, to make sure all was as it should be before rejoining the others. But as she opened the door, she knew all was not as it should be.

A margarita glass lay smashed on the floor amid a pool of blood. The air was tinged with a coppery smell. The tables so carefully draped in white linen cloths were spattered with red. And if those things didn't indicate that the memorial luncheon that Daisy had worked so hard on was about to be ruined, then the body lying in the middle of the room left no doubt.

"Oh, dear," she whispered as she backed out, closing the door behind her. "I guess Shirley isn't going to make it to Archie's memorial."

CHAPTER THREE

$\mathcal{A}$fter stationing herself before the doors of the solarium, Araminta borrowed a cellphone from one of the younger Moorecliffs in residence and placed the call to 911 herself. There would be havoc aplenty once the police arrived, but she wanted none of it now. She needed to secure the area.

Luckily, the solarium was filled with lush plants this season. Yancy had really outdone himself. There were tall flowers, bunches of decorative grasses, and vines obscuring most of the interior view from the windows.

On the lawn, most of the guests were loitering behind, listening to the excitement pouring from the currently reigning Moorecliff matriarch as she led the group toward the special garden section she'd had created in remembrance of the wonderful man who had been her husband.

Poor Daisy, she thought. Araminta knew this was going to break her heart. She had worked so hard to set up a memorial to celebrate her late husband's life. Now here they were, about to face yet another murder.

Half an hour later, she was speaking with Detective Ivan Hershey—the same detective who had handled the investigation of Archie's murder. Word had gotten out about Cousin Shirley, and an anxious crowd had gathered. As Araminta had guessed from the amount of blood, Shirley had been stabbed, but there was no murder weapon at the scene.

However, Arun had zipped straight into the solarium the moment the cops opened the doors, with Sasha right behind him. One of them had found an important clue: a bloodied gardening glove.

"Oh, my! The gardener's glove?" someone whispered. "But… wasn't she having a thing with him?"

"No, that was years ago," someone else replied.

"I heard as soon as they saw each other again,

the whole relationship was rekindled."

Ivan looked at Araminta, and she knew without a doubt that he, too, had heard the whispered conversation. He turned to Daisy. "We need to speak to the gardener, Ms. Moorecliff. Can you have him come down here?"

She lowered her gaze then shook her head. "Yancy isn't here this morning, I'm afraid. He requested the day off, and I gave it to him since—well, since the work in the memorial garden was done. But he couldn't possibly be involved…"

Araminta handed her a handkerchief. "Of course he isn't involved. And his absence is not an admission of guilt. No one expected what happened here, Daisy. Especially given the reason we are all here—we are in mourning, for heaven's sake! What could the killer have been thinking?"

"To shut her up, maybe," came another whisper from the crowd, catching Ivan's attention.

"Shirley talked a lot?" he asked, his pen hovering over the little paper tablet he held in his hand. Araminta bit back a smile. Unlike the other cops, apparently, Ivan preferred a good old-fashioned paper and pen to electronics. It must have been something he learned from his grandfather, who had come to stand beside him.

Jacob Hershey was retired from the police force now, but he and Araminta had gone a few rounds over investigations back in the day. Old-school, Jacob would call it, and he wasn't wrong. When he was on the force, paper and pen were all they'd had —or pencil, now that she thought about it. That, and a telephone.

"Of course she talked a lot, boy! Shirley was the gossip of the family, and she never learned to curb that tongue of hers, if there's truth to what I've been hearing," Jacob Hershey said then nodded to the ladies. "Hello, Daisy. I am sorry about what happened to Archie. He was a good man. Better than most. Sad he can no longer be with us."

To Araminta, he said nothing. Instead, he directed his comments to Ivan. "Keep your eye on this one, boy. She likes to butt her nose in. To interfere."

His voice was gruff, and Araminta knew the grit in his tone was not owing entirely to his age. His gaze was cautious, though he continued to stand his ground, even after Araminta's eyes narrowed. She wouldn't stand for his aspersions against her character, not now, but she didn't mind casting one against his. "Wouldn't have to if you did your job, Jacob.

How many clues would you have missed if I hadn't been there?"

Ivan stepped in before their discussion could become heated. "Ms. Moorecliff is a lovely woman, Grandfather. I'd be delighted to have her assistance —especially after the help she provided in solving the late Mr. Moorecliff's murder. Now, if you'll excuse us, I have more questions for Araminta."

He held out his arm for her, and Araminta took it, but not before shooting a victory smile over her shoulder at Jacob. "I am happy to assist, Detective, in whatever manner I can."

"Tell me about Shirley Moorecliff. Talk says she knew a bit about everyone's habits. What do you know of hers?"

Araminta sighed. "It has been a while since we've spent time together, as you might have guessed. The Moorecliff clan is pretty large these days. It takes something momentous or equally horrid to bring us all together."

"She was a cousin?" he asked as they walked toward the house.

Araminta noticed he kept looking around as if searching for something. "Detective, I believe Miss Stephanie went back inside the house as soon as we left Daisy."

He flushed but neither affirmed nor denied her guess that he was looking for Stephanie. "Shirley had a sister. Olive, I believe. I spoke to her earlier."

"Yes." Araminta nodded. "Olive and Shirley are Walter's children. The pair of them used to stay at the manor, and even then, they got into all sorts of mischief."

"And did that mischief include the gardener?"

Araminta hesitated. She didn't want to be the one to point fingers at Yancy, but she couldn't lie. "If memory serves, Shirley did have a thing for Yancy. But there were quite a few cousins—and even Shirley's sister, Olive—that had flirtations with him. He was quite the thing back then."

Hershey made a note then nodded. "Thank you for your time, Ms. Moorecliff. I'll be in touch."

As the detective drove off along the lane leading up to Moorecliff Manor, a delivery van arrived. "Another arrangement of flowers for Daisy, I presume?" Araminta asked Stephanie, who had answered the doorbell since Harold hadn't heard it.

Stephanie nodded. "Roses today."

Araminta watched the delivery van drive out of sight. "So I suppose it'll be the wildflowers again tomorrow."

CHAPTER FOUR

*A*run pushed his paw gently against the acorn. He looked up, measuring the distance to the gap in the hedges, then pulled his paw back and shot forward. The acorn skittered across the pavers and slid through the gap. "Score!"

Sasha frowned, the dark hair on her forehead wrinkling above her sky-blue eyes. "Fine. You beat me. But I was the one who found the glove."

She flopped down on the warm patch of sun that filtered through the tall oak tree and started grooming, losing interest in the game they'd been playing, as she usually did when losing. She wasn't very competitive, except when it came to investigating mysteries.

"You found it, but I led the humans." Arun was proud of his ability to bring the humans to the clues. "And we're lucky I did. Who knows how long it would have taken them on their own?"

"Araminta would have found it quickly, I'm sure. That Ivan Hershey, I'm not so sure he would have."

"He doesn't appear to be as astute as his grand-father," Arun agreed. "Jacob would have noticed it right away."

"Maybe they should call us in as consultants."

Arun snorted. "We'd break the cases in record time."

"No doubt." Sasha licked a paw and pushed it behind her ear as the two cats retreated into their own thoughts about the various cases they'd helped solve.

"There are still plenty of clues to uncover in this one." Arun stood, his gaze drifting over to the solarium, where the police were still searching and conducting interviews. "Perhaps we should get to work."

Sasha sighed. "I suppose."

"I want to listen in and perhaps search the guest rooms for clues."

Sasha perked up. She loved searching the

rooms. "Yes, and don't forget we have to alert Araminta to our latest find."

"Of course, I can't wait for her to see what is going on in the gardening shed," Arun said.

Sasha looked over her shoulder at him as she trotted ahead. "And don't forget what I found when we were playing hide-and-seek behind the draperies in Shirley's room. That will certainly be of interest in this case."

With the police busy interviewing the guests and searching the grounds for whatever murder weapon the killer had used to dispense with Shirley, Araminta decided it was time to take a look in the gardening shed.

The cats must have sensed her direction, because they trotted along in front of her, glancing back in the way that cats do when they pretend to be leading while they are actually following. At least she thought they were following, though she had to admit it did appear as if they thought *she* was following *them*.

Due to the bloodstained gardening glove near

the body, it made sense the cops would suspect Yancy, the Moorecliffs' gardener. But Araminta knew things were rarely so cut-and-dried. She wasn't sure if the police had searched the shed yet, but it couldn't hurt to have a look herself in case there was something they had missed. Maybe there was something to be found in the little building out back that would shed some light on the subject.

The building dated to her grandfather's time and sat in the back of the property, where the grounds were still covered with trees, shrubs, and a lot of underbrush. There was a clear path through it all to the quaint little building, which, of course, she and the cats made sure to follow. Since Araminta didn't know who'd killed Shirley or why they had done so, she would take care. Somewhere out there, a killer was running loose, and she had no wish whatsoever to become the next victim.

From the outside, the building looked quite like a small weathered cabin in the woods, though the inside was home to Yancy's equipment, his fertilizers and plant foods, a handful or two of specialized gardening books, and of course, his tools—spades, snips, trimmers, and whatnot. Araminta only hoped she didn't also find the murder weapon.

The cats, of course, made it to the shack ahead

of her, and they did not look happy about whatever they'd found, prancing and yowling in front of the door to the shed as they were. Araminta knew they were trying to get her attention. As soon as she got close, she knew why. The door was cracked open slightly. Was the killer inside? Was that the reason the cats were kicking up such a fuss?

She glanced back over her shoulder, indecisive. Should she call down to the solarium for the police to come back around?

Before she could make her decision, Arun gave a loud meow and bolted inside. Araminta knew she would have to go in to collect him. Sasha, at least, waited for her. Araminta reached down to give her a pat in thanks for her patience before they walked into the building together. "Good girl. Good girl," she told the cat, her voice low, in case someone was lurking beyond the door.

Inside, the building wasn't quite a shambles, but the contents of the shed were in clear disarray, as if everything had been pushed to one side to make a bit of room for—something. With gossip being that Yancy and Shirley had rekindled their old love affair, Araminta didn't want to even think of what might have gone on here. Instead, she poked around fallen tools and stacks of bags, not sure for what, exactly, she was looking.

After a moment, Arun sent up a yowl. He'd found something. Araminta hurried to see what and discovered a few articles of clothing in the corner. Kneeling, she picked up each piece and examined it thoroughly. Were these Yancy's? She wasn't sure, but it was obvious none of the clothes were Shirley's—thank goodness! There were smears of grass and dirt on all of the items, but at least none of it was bloodied like the glove the cats had found.

Araminta placed the soiled items of clothing in a pile. She would send Harold or Trinity to fetch it for laundering later. For now, she knew she should get back to the house. Daisy would need her help dealing with the many Moorecliffs in residence, especially after what had happened.

Outside again, Araminta squinted at the door. When she and the cats arrived, that door was already open—but why? Yancy had been given the day off, so there was no reason he should have been in here this morning. If he truly was responsible for Shirley's murder, he must have done it last night.

But the door had been open…

Had he come to take the murder weapon away

and then left in such a rush he'd forgotten to properly close it behind him?

Pulling the door shut, Araminta made sure it clicked into place, then she walked away from the shed, a heavy sigh spilling from her lips. She dearly hoped Yancy was not found to be the killer. Like Harold, Trinity, and Mary the cook, the gardener was practically one of the family. Not to mention, he didn't seem the murdering type.

Yancy was a man of dedication, she decided. Just look what he had managed to accomplish in a short amount of time. Daisy had given him a scant few weeks to transform that corner of the garden near the solarium, and though he'd had a bit of help, he had completed the project in record time.

From the talk she'd heard among the other staff members, he was even given to a bit of philanthropy. He gave his time two days a week as a volunteer down at the homeless shelter. Was it possible for a man like that to be capable of such a brutal murder?

Araminta didn't want to believe it of him, but she had seen the glove the cats had found in the grass outside the solarium. It belonged to the gardener, and Yancy did have sharp tools with which to commit the crime, so he certainly had a method. Given his supposed rekindled affair with the victim, he also had ample opportunity. One thing puzzled Araminta and made her more than a little doubtful Shirley's murderer was the Moorecliffs' gardener: if he loved Shirley, then why would he kill her?

CHAPTER FIVE

Sure the police would have found something by now, Araminta made her way back along the wooded path to the memorial garden, the cats following along beside her. She was halfway there when she saw Olive Moorecliff headed in her direction.

Olive and Shirley were sisters, but each had a different mother. Walter Moorecliff's first wife had passed on after Olive's birth. She had died of complications. Then Walter had remarried shortly after, and Shirley had come along about a year later. There had been talk at the time about a lack of proper mourning, but Walter hadn't cared about wagging tongues. He'd loved his first wife, and he'd loved his second. He'd just wanted to get on with his life.

Early on, Shirley and Olive had been nearly inseparable, but as teens, they'd had their share of squabbles. Still, they must have remained close. Olive was a mess, practically beside herself with anguish. "Olive? Olive, darling, are you all right?"

Tears were streaming down her face, and though she nodded, Araminta decided perhaps it was best if they walked back to the house together so the two of them could talk about it. Sometimes it helped if one had a shoulder to lean on—and maybe Olive would know for sure if there was truly anything going on between her sister and Yancy.

"What do I do, Minty? What do I do?" she asked, wringing her hands all the while.

"About what?" Araminta asked.

"Shirley!" she bawled. "We had a falling out a long time ago, you know? We got by after, but we grew so far apart. We never truly reconciled!"

So that was what had her so torn up, was it? Araminta put her arm across Olive's shoulder and patted her arm in an effort to console her. "There, there, dry your eyes, Olive. I am sure your sister knows you wanted to. The two of you were like twins."

"Maybe," Olive murmured. "But we could have reconciled. Up until this morning, we could have."

She closed her eyes, and the tears started again. "Now we will never have the chance."

After a moment of silence, Olive took a deep breath and dried her eyes. "But Shirley isn't the reason I came up here after you. I—I could use some advice."

"Advice?" Apparently, the cats didn't want to wait around for Olive to pull herself together. The pair of them strutted down the path, tails in the air.

Arun glanced back as if to say, "Are you coming?" She could practically see the frown on his velvety brown mask. If the cats were that interested in something up ahead, she sure wanted to see what it was. It could be a clue. But then Olive turned her attention back to the conversation with her next words.

"Yes, you see, I—I think I saw something."

Araminta's senses went immediately on alert. "Something relevant to Shirley's murder, you mean?"

Olive shrugged. "I'm not sure. But the police are asking questions of everyone, and I was wondering if you think I should tell the police what I saw outside my room last night?"

Araminta considered it. "Perhaps you should tell me first. Then together, we can decide if you should go to the police. Did you see Shirley with someone last night?"

"No, no." Olive batted away the possibility with the hand in which she held the handkerchief. "It's Owen. You know our rooms are next door to one another, right?"

Araminta nodded. "Yes, but I don't see how the location of his room could be relevant…"

Olive leaned near as if to share a deep confidence. "I saw Angie sneaking in there last night!"

Araminta's eyes widened at the news, but she was not truly shocked. Everyone in the family knew Angie had only married David for his money. But Owen? Really? He was David's brother, for crying out loud, and as poor as a church mouse, to boot. She shook her head. "Only Angie would stoop to an affair with her brother-in-law."

"It's horrid, I tell you! But should I tell the police what I know? I mean, it is suspicious behavior, after all—right?"

Araminta started to say yes, it was suspiciously despicable behavior, but Olive cut her off.

"I'm sure Shirley must have known about it too. Do you think she was planning to use Angie's affair with Owen for her own advantage? I mean, I don't want to get Angie into any sort of trouble, but——"

"I think we will keep this to ourselves for the time being, Olive. An affair is more of a family scandal kind of thing in this instance."

"But it could have been motive for murder, right? If Shirley knew about Owen and Angie, either one of them might have wanted to keep her quiet to make sure David never found out."

Araminta had to admit she did have a point. But if Angie and Owen's affair was outed and neither of them was guilty of murder, why, that news would ruin quite a few innocent lives. "You could be right, Olive. You could certainly be right. But what if you're not? We have to consider what this would do to David and Angie's children before we just blurt it all out into the open."

"I can barely allow myself to imagine one of them could be Shirley's killer, but you're right."

Araminta nodded, thankful Olive seemed in agreement to keep her secrets to herself for the moment.

"I will leave it to you, Araminta. I know you are good at these sorts of things." Olive's eyes misted over again. "I need to make sure Shirley's death is avenged. It's the last thing I can do for her."

"I promise that will happen." Araminta would do her best to find the killer, but accusing someone in the family was a delicate matter. If Angie or Owen was Shirley's murderer, she needed proof beyond a shadow of a doubt.

ack at the manor, Araminta saw the police had finally removed the body and sealed off the solarium. Some of the uniformed officers were searching the manor, and there was still a handful of guests to question, but soon, they'd be on their way.

Daisy had already given them a list of all the guests, along with their contact information in case they needed to speak with someone again. Shirley had clearly been stabbed, but until they got the results from the autopsy with more details about what kind of knife or tool they were really looking for, there wasn't much else they could do here.

Araminta, on the other hand, didn't have time for the badges to finish their work and leave.

Someone had killed another Moorecliff family member, and she meant to find out who.

Following the cats upstairs, she looked first one way and then the other at the long, double row of doors. Family was staying in many of those typically unused chambers, but someone among them had killed Shirley. Searching all the rooms would be a task, but it was possible the police had missed something when they were up here. The question was, where to start?

Arun solved that dilemma for her. He raced straight to Shirley's room. He meowed until Sasha joined him, and they both sat, waiting for Araminta to open the door. Inside, Araminta shook her head. The cops had practically turned this room inside out, and she could only assume there would be more of the same kind of disarray in all the others.

Meow.

Arun was standing by the window, looking up at Araminta. She hurried over. From here, she could see the guests still milling about in the garden. She could see the solarium too. Had Shirley stood here, looking down into the gardens, keeping an eye on her lover?

Meow!

Distracted from her thoughts, Araminta looked down. "What is it, Arun?"

The cat dipped his head into the folds of the drapery then nudged at the material with his paw. Araminta finally saw what he was obviously trying to show her. There was a small slip of paper in the hem of the drapery. She could see only the corner of it, peeking out from the opening where a few stitches had come undone. The old draperies really did need to be replaced.

"You've found something already?" Curious, she bent to retrieve it, but Arun stopped her before she could touch the paper. "Right. Don't need to get my prints on there."

Using the hem of her blouse, she lifted the paper from where it must have fallen and become hidden in the heavy folds of fabric after Shirley read it. It was easy to see how the police had missed it, tucked into the hem and facing the wall. Who would think to look there? Arun and Sasha, on the other hand, loved hiding behind drapes and some-times even climbing them.

There was a single line of text on the sheet. *Midnight in the solarium*, it said. Someone had given Shirley a note to lure her into the solarium! Was it from Yancy, after all? Had he sent Shirley this note to have her meet him for a midnight fling? Or was it intended to lure his one-time lover to her death? How long had the note been there? No one had occupied the room for over a year, but the note could be from then or before. Maybe it had nothing to do with Shirley… but Araminta didn't think so.

Studying the note carefully, Araminta paid attention to every detail, committing it all to memory, because she would need to surrender what she had found to the cops.

The writing was old-school, as Jacob Hershey would say. Cursive, with lovely, flowing letters. Open loops. Nothing closed up tightly. If the handwriting analysis course of study she'd taken online had a bit of substance to it, she could surmise that whoever had written this note had felt they had nothing to hide. Or maybe they'd believed no one would find it, so there was no chance of them getting caught?

The paper was plain white with no ruled lines on it. It looked very common. No clues there.

The cats seemed satisfied there was nothing more to be found in this room, so Araminta slipped the note into her pocket and headed back downstairs to take it to the authorities still searching for whatever the killer had used to murder Shirley.

At the foot of the stairs, she saw Ivan speaking with Stephanie. "Detective Hershey, I thought you'd gone?"

He straightened and stepped away from her grandniece. "Yes, there was another call, unfortunately, but I hurried back the moment it was done."

"Hmph." Hurried, indeed, Araminta thought. Clearly, he'd come back to speak with Stephanie. And from the smile on that one's face, she didn't seem to mind. "Well, since you are here, I shall give this to you. I found this in Shirley's room. It was hiding in the hem of the drapes. What do you make of it?"

With her finger and thumb once more draped by the hem of her blouse, Araminta fished the handwritten note from her pocket.

Hershey snapped on a glove and took it from her. His eyes narrowed as he read. "Clearly someone wanted your relative to be in the solarium."

"Yes, precisely." Araminta put her hands on her hips and sighed. "But why?"

"That does seem to be the question, doesn't it?" Folding the paper, Hershey slipped it into an evidence bag. "All that remains is to find the answer."

CHAPTER SEVEN

*D*inner that night was a raucous affair, to say the least. As Trinity and Harold did their part to make sure everyone's goblets remained filled along with their bellies, the conversation at every table focused on what had happened to Shirley.

The general consensus among the family seemed to be that Shirley must have gone too far. Everyone knew that she had a habit of using what she knew against people. In short, she was nosy, and her tongue was venomous. Plus, she had trouble keeping her mouth shut.

Those few who weren't voicing various speculations about Shirley and her noisome habit of keeping tabs on all the family's secrets were equally grumbling and commiserating with Daisy over what a shame it was to have all that wasted food just sitting there in the solarium. With the room sealed off by the police while they investigated Shirley Moorecliff's murder, all the beautiful, catered dishes Daisy had ordered in for the affair would have to be discarded.

"Guess there will be a lot more mice in the walls after this fiasco than there already are. They'll soon be teeming, with that much food to share between them," Prudence Abernathy piped up. Her voice was overly loud, her expression full of judgement. Her fear of mice in the house must not have dulled her appetite, though, judging by the load of food balanced on the silver fork she had clutched in her left hand. Araminta knew she had raised her voice to ensure there was no way her hostess would not hear her.

Daisy gasped at her blatant accusation of household mismanagement, but somehow managed to hang on to her composure. Araminta silently applauded her delicate aplomb as Daisy calmly folded her napkin and laid it carefully over the purse in her lap before she spoke.

"Mice? At Moorecliff Manor? I think not, my dear. Surely, you are mistaken!"

Prudence—or Pru, as most of the family called her—used her fork to move her food from one side of her plate to the other. Her brow rose, and she tilted her head to the side, but she continued to play with her dinner as she smirked. "My ears hear what they hear, darling. Those nasty rodents woke me early this morning. There must be hundreds of them, because they were so loud, I couldn't finish my sleep."

Araminta leaned forward in her chair. "I suppose lack of sleep is to blame for your current mood? Eat your dinner, Pru. You sound cranky and more than a bit petulant. Much like a child, actually."

Prudence dropped her fork and glared at Araminta. "There are mice in the walls, I tell you. If you are content to reside with those nasty, beady-eyed rodents, so be it. For myself, I'm out of this ancient pile of planks the moment this dastardly investigation is through."

At the head of the table, Daisy had gone white, but this time, her pallor was not due to the recent murder. Rather, Araminta could see she was beside herself with indignation that someone had dared cast aspersions on her home-management skills. Araminta steeled herself for what was coming—

from the look on Daisy's face, there was about to be an explosion.

Beside her, Robert Blakely murmured, "Don't worry that anyone will miss you."

Araminta suppressed a chuckle and turned again to step in with Prudence. "There's no reason for your impertinence, woman. Daisy keeps Moorecliff Manor in tip-top shape. With the help of Harold and Trinity and Yancy, of course. If there were mice, we would know. Of that, I can personally assure you."

Beaten at her childish little game meant to besmirch Daisy, Prudence pushed back her chair and immediately left the room. The minute she was gone, a semblance of normal conversation resumed.

"You must feel crushed to have all your efforts with the memorial gone to waste," Olive told Daisy. "Especially that beautiful cake! I never dreamed someone would have the skills to create such a detailed Moorecliff motorcar replica."

Araminta frowned as she thought of all the food. They'd spent hours choosing what to serve and having the caterer make various items. Finger sandwiches in tiered trays. Deviled eggs in those cute little platters with egg-shaped indents. Desserts galore. So much food that she hadn't even gotten a chance to preview the cakes. Maybe she could check out the motorcar cake before the police took it all away. She had to admit Daisy had cleverly stuck to the motorcar theme with whatever she could. Now all that food was contaminated and had to be tossed. Such a waste.

Soon, dinner drew to an end, and everyone began to wander away from the dining room in favor of a rest upstairs. Araminta chose to loiter with her cats in the parlor. After what Olive had told her earlier about Owen and his sister-in-law, she wanted to have a few words with Angie.

Not that it made sense to her that Angie might be Shirley's murderer. The fact that she and Owen were having an affair, practically under her husband's nose, didn't mean Angie would want to kill anyone over it. Unless she felt threatened by exposure, of course. Had Shirley made such a threat to her?

Everyone in the family knew Angie had married not for love, but for money, and she certainly would not want to relinquish what access to it her marriage had given her. Araminta wasn't positive that Shirley had blackmailed members of the family before, but she'd heard the rumors. And if Shirley had blackmailed them, it was unlikely anyone would admit to it.

Now, how to approach Angie? Araminta couldn't come right out and accuse her of infidelity. Surely she would deny that, and it wouldn't make her eager to talk to Araminta. A subtle approach would be best. If she and Owen were sneaking around in the halls at night, maybe one of the two had seen something?

Araminta stroked the kitties while she waited in the parlor. One way or the other, she meant to find out what she could to determine whether or not Shirley's killer was Owen or Angie.

CHAPTER EIGHT

Angela "Angie" Moorecliff was a shrewd woman and a good actress. Though Araminta knew the rumor of her only marrying for money was true, Angie hid it well, especially from her husband. Only the keenest observers of human behavior would notice the subtle hints that she was more in love with the money than the man.

Angie's love of material wealth showed in her choices and in her lifestyle. She wore the latest fashions from the day's top designers. She wore the costliest perfumes, had only the best stylists in the country tend her hair, and spent more time jet-setting around the world on the yacht her husband's money had paid for than she did lounging around their million-dollar home on the west coast. She was always in the company of men who she claimed to be "just friends."

This evening, she was dressed, yet again, to the nines, from the dangling diamonds sparkling at her ears to the cream-chiffon polish gracing her toes. Araminta caught her on her way out of the dining room. She was walking at her husband's side, but it was her brother-in-law, Owen, at whom she smiled.

"Angie, dear, how lovely to see you! We've hardly had a chance to chat since you arrived!" Araminta tugged at Angie's arm to separate her from the herd.

Araminta noted the way Angie's gaze became hooded for just a second before she turned to speak to her husband, but she'd added an unnecessary bit of volume to her tone. Araminta felt sure she'd wanted Owen, not her husband, to hear her. "Do go on ahead of me, darling. I will catch up later."

She turned to Araminta with her faux smile. "Yes, dear, how can I help you?" Her gaze drifted down to Araminta's outfit. "Some fashion advice, perhaps?"

Araminta smoothed her jacket. Sure, her clothing choices were a bit unconventional, but she liked them much better than Angela's flashy style. "Not this time."

Araminta steered her over to a small unoccupied sitting room so they could talk in private. She took a seat in a mahogany carved Victorian chair that had belonged to her grandfather and been recently reupholstered in rose brocade and gestured for Angie to take the matching chair next to her.

The chairs were out of the way and out of earshot of anyone in the main hall. They were also set in the corner and positioned so that Araminta could see anyone approaching—a perfect spot for a subtle interrogation.

"So, dear, how have you and David been getting on? And Karen and Douglass, are they doing well?" Araminta opened by asking about Angie's children. People loved to talk about their kids, and it usually made them drop their guard. Angie was no exception.

"They're doing great. Thanks for asking." As Angie went on to gush about her children's latest accomplishments, Araminta feigned intense interest, nodding and smiling, and saying things like "That's wonderful!" at all the right times as she considered how best to get the information she needed from Angie.

The cats also seemed interested. As Angie talked, they circled her ankles. Angie didn't seem to enjoy their attention, her lips pursed and hands shooing at them every so often. She probably didn't want cat fur on her expensive outfit. The cats, of course, sensed this and proceeded to rub up against her as much as possible.

Finally, there was a break in her monologue, and Araminta was able to start her inquiry. "And how have you and David been sleeping here at the manor? I do hope it's not too noisy." Araminta leaned forward and lowered her voice. "I don't believe that there are mice in the walls, but I do believe one of the staff saw you walking about. I hope nothing has kept you awake."

Angie stiffened. "The staff saw me? No, they must be mistaken."

So that was how she was going to play it? Denial? Araminta would have to play hardball. She didn't have time to waste. "Are you sure? I do believe someone said they saw you in the hallway near Owen's room. I was wondering what you would be doing there."

"Who? Who said that?" Angie stuttered, her composure faltering.

"It's not important. The thing is, there's been a murder, and the police are questioning people. Now you wouldn't want them to find out about your nightly excursions, would you?" Araminta leaned forward. "So tell me, were you with Owen around two a.m. this morning?"

Angie gasped. "You—oh, you think I killed *Shirley*? How dare you!" Her dander was definitely up. "You're as bad as she was—a nosy old busybody! Why don't you look to your own family, huh? Before you cast your malicious stones at me!"

Araminta's brows drew together. "I don't know what you mean."

Angie's eyes narrowed at Araminta. She confessed, "Yes, I was with Owen in his room this morning, but I wasn't the only one wandering around Moorecliff Manor."

Araminta's focus sharpened. "You saw someone else?"

Angie nodded and crossed her arms over her chest, her expression smug now that she had something to bargain with. "Several people, in fact. Some who are very close to you."

Araminta didn't like the way this was going. "Like who?"

"Well for one, that sourpuss Prudence Abernathy was in the hallway, making one of her many trips to the bathroom." Angie's scowl deepened. "She's the one that told on me, isn't she?"

"I can't really say." Araminta, not wanting to put the finger on Olive, let Angie think what she wanted. "But I'm not particularly close to Prudence."

"She's not the only one. But she was acting a bit strange. I know she's getting on in years and has to make many trips to the bathroom at night, but when I turned the corner, I saw her looking around the hallway as if she was confused. I jumped back of course, since I didn't want to be noticed, but I swear she was coming out of the hall closet, not the bathroom." Angie chuckled. "You might want to have the maid check the closet to be sure Prudence hasn't gone senile and used the wrong room."

Araminta made a face as she considered Pru as the killer. Had Shirley had something on her? Was that why she kept talking about the mice? Were the mice some sort of misdirection to hide the fact that she was the killer?

"Anyway, I'm not the killer, and I'm sure you will want to keep my nocturnal journeys to yourself after you hear who else I saw sneaking around."

Apparently, Shirley wasn't the only family member who was into blackmail—Angie was now using it to guarantee Araminta's silence, which made her very nervous about the answer to her next question. "Who?"

Angie smirked. "I saw Stephanie sneaking in the back door by the kitchen. Why would she be doing that if she had nothing to hide? Like I said, maybe you should be keeping that eagle eye of yours on the members of your own family instead of mine."

Stephanie was wandering the manor in the early hours of the morning? Araminta felt a bit of a chill. Steph hadn't been down to the table for dinner this evening, either, and now Araminta was worried about why. Stephanie had developed a keen interest in gardening lately, and Araminta was sure something had been going on in the gardening shed.

"I will speak to her about that."

Angie nodded and stood but then hesitated before taking her leave. "You will keep the details of this conversation to yourself, then? David has no idea about Owen…"

Araminta wondered how that could possibly be true, but David had never been known for his powers of observation. He'd always been rather oblivious, a geeky nerd with his head in the clouds and a brain focused on numbers. That was how he'd made millions in investments.

Angela tapped her foot nervously. She really was worried Araminta might tell him and her gravy train would dry up. But even though David didn't notice, it didn't mean that others were oblivious. Olive had noticed. Had Shirley? This was something Shirley would certainly take advantage of.

If Shirley knew and was blackmailing Angela, that would be a compelling motive for murder. And here Angela was, casting suspicion away from herself by claiming she'd seen Stephanie.

Araminta assured Angie of her silence with a nod. "I won't say a word, but perhaps you could practice being a bit more circumspect? As you know, some in the family are more watchful of the habits of others, and with more malicious intent. They tend to focus on the gritty, dirty details."

Angela let a breath out and managed to look humble. "Thank you."

Araminta shooed her on her way. "Go on. Your secret is safe."

Angie nodded and walked away toward the parlor door, halting only briefly when Araminta said, "Thank you for telling me about Stephanie."

"Any time," she murmured over her shoulder, her voice more cold than sincere.

Araminta remained in the chair, thinking about

what she'd just learned. Sasha leapt into her lap and she stroked her silky fur for comfort. Angela was a liar, but Araminta didn't think she'd lied about Stephanie. Araminta would have to confront her grandniece soon.

And what about Prudence? Had she really been in the closet, or was Angie wrong about where she'd seen her coming from? Had Pru just been confused about which door led to the bathroom, or was she up to something too?

Araminta glanced at her watch. Her gaze slid to the hallway, which led to the kitchen and the door Steph had apparently slipped in through after most of the family were in their rooms sleeping last night.

Images of the murder scene bubbled up. Shirley had definitely been stabbed, but had it been with one of the knives from that very kitchen? The police had yet to release those details.

As Araminta headed upstairs, a question nagged. Where was Stephanie now? The girl hadn't come down for dinner, although such an occurrence would have been unheard of a few weeks ago, before Archie died. The Moorecliff family dined together, no matter how many members were in residence. So why was Stephanie bucking tradition at this particular time?

CHAPTER NINE

Araminta paced the sitting room that adjoined to her bedroom in her house shoes, robe, and gown. After her chat with Angie, she had gone upstairs to check if her grandniece was in her rooms, but she hadn't been there. That had been around a quarter past nine.

The old clock on her mantel chimed midnight, and Araminta stepped close to peer out the window at the gardens below. At midnight, Stephanie still hadn't returned to the manor. Stephanie was young and liked to stay out late with her friends, but Araminta would have thought that considering the recent death of her father and even-more-recent murder at the mansion, Stephanie would have stuck closer to home. Hopefully, there wasn't a more sinister reason that Stephanie was not in her room. Not that Araminta thought Stephanie capable of murder, but Steph had become close with Yancy, and Yancy was a prime suspect. Was she hiding Yancy or abetting him somehow?

Luckily, only Angela had seen Stephanie, and Araminta doubted Angie would tell the police, because it might expose her secret affair. But the question of Stephanie's whereabouts and reason for going began to plague Araminta to the point that even the cats had begun to fidget nervously beneath her regard.

Araminta paced her room, thoughts whirling. She barely noticed the cats trailing her, trotting behind her step for step, curling around her feet as they were wont to do, until Sasha raced over to the window and jumped up on the wide windowsill to stare out into the night.

Outside, the tall oak tree loomed in the dark. Araminta's gaze fell to the dark patch of mulch beneath. A patch of lily of the valley flowers had been planted there once, but since they'd been used to poison her husband, Daisy had had them ripped out.

Meow!

Arun jumped up onto the sill and head-butted

Araminta's hand then looked out the window. Both cats appeared to be in deep concentration, their blue eyes staring, delicate ears pointed forward. They weren't looking up at the moon or the stars as they usually did but toward the tree. Were they thinking about the lily of the valley flowers too? But no… they weren't looking down. They were looking straight ahead.

Araminta put on her glasses and squinted. Was that the yellow glow of a light? Someone was out there. She leaned close, peering deep into the shadows where she'd last seen the flickers. A dim glow seemed to be coming from the gardener's shed.

Had Yancy returned without telling anyone? Or could it be Stephanie out there in the woods?

It must be Yancy. Perhaps he had heard something? Was there more trouble brewing? Had he heard or seen something he was now investigating to try to clear his name? Or worse, if he were truly the killer, was he preparing to take down another Moorecliff?

After a few seconds of rummaging around in the middle drawer of her writing desk, Araminta found the small flashlight she kept there for emergencies or in case the electricity should go out in the middle of the night and she needed to be able to find her way to the ground floor of the manor. "Come on, kitties, but be silent, if you please. We are going out there to have a look around, but I'd rather not alert whoever is skulking around the grounds to our presence in case it's Shirley's killer."

Jacob Hershey would have a fit if he knew what she was about to do. He would chastise her for not thinking before she hustled out and give a stern warning about what was and wasn't smart. Araminta knew well enough there could be trouble in the dark, but Stephanie was out there somewhere, and she couldn't just stay inside. What if the girl should need her help?

Using the back stairs because they offered the quickest route to the back door off the kitchen, Araminta made as little noise as possible while hurrying toward the garden shed. If there was an intruder inside… well, she'd rather not think of that.

Cautiously, Araminta made a motion with her hand to her lips for the cats to keep silent as she approached the shed. Opening the door, she poked the flashlight inside and had a quick look around. Someone had definitely been in there! More clothing was heaped in one corner, along with a bit of food she knew had come from what was left untouched in the solarium. She was about to step inside when she noticed a shadow looming behind her. Her hand froze on the door, and her heart practically leapt from her chest.

Dropping the flashlight, Araminta took a moment to recall something she'd learned in her younger days and spun around to face her would-be attacker, assuming her best remembered karate stance. If she was going to have to fight off a killer, she meant to let him or her know she'd come prepared. But…

"Auntie?"

Araminta could hardly believe her eyes "Reginald? What in the world are you doing here? You're supposed to be at the Gamblers Anonymous retreat."

Reggie simply stood and stared at her. Maybe he was too shocked by finding her in here to speak, or maybe he needed time to come up with an excuse. Either way, it didn't bode well. Why would Reggie be living out here, unless he had something to hide?

Araminta's thoughts went to Shirley. She was very good at digging up everyone's secrets and taking advantage. Had she found out about

Reggie's problem and blackmailed him? Hadn't one of the other relatives alluded to that very thing?

If Araminta hadn't known her nephew so well, she might have been suspicious. Reggie had come up with the perfect alibi by not coming to the memorial. Had he skipped the retreat and come back to kill Shirley? And if so, why was he still hanging around?

CHAPTER TEN

Glancing around as if he were afraid someone else may have followed Araminta to the gardener's shed, Reggie picked up the flashlight she had dropped and urged her inside. "I apologize, Aunt Minty, but I couldn't miss Father's memorial."

Araminta speared him with a look. "So you skipped out on the Gamblers Anonymous retreat? After all your stepmother has done for you? The debt she paid? You made a promise, Reginald."

Arun and Sasha raced to Reggie's side as if to provide comfort from Araminta's scolding.

Head bowed, probably because he knew what she'd said was true and he was feeling a little ashamed of himself, Reggie nodded. "That's why

I've been staying out here. I was just going to watch from afar. I didn't want to hurt her, so I figured if she didn't know…"

He bent down to scoop up Arun and cuddled him while Sasha stood on her hind legs, batting at his knee for attention.

Araminta sighed. At least now she understood why there was clothing and food here, even though Yancy hadn't been on the premises.

"But that hasn't stopped you from lurking about, peeking into windows, has it now?" Araminta fussed. Hands on her hips, she narrowed her eyes, though she doubted he would get the full effect. It would be difficult to see her expression in here since there was only a tiny bit of moonlight coming in through the windows and Reggie had his face buried in the cat's fur. "It was you I saw peering through the window to the dining room this morning, wasn't it?"

With reluctance, he confessed. "Yes. I wanted to at least see the cousins, although I knew I would not be able to speak with any of them, not that I minded that too much. Still, it is good to *see* them. And then the police came, and I had to disappear to keep from being noticed. What happened?"

"Shirley was killed. Found her in the solarium

when we all walked down to celebrate and commemorate your father's life."

"The family gossip? *That* Shirley?" Reggie put Arun down and squatted to give Sasha her share of attention.

Araminta nodded. "The same."

Looking around the shed again, though she had already done so earlier in the day, Araminta asked, "Have you seen Yancy? Daisy told us earlier she had given him the day off."

Reginald shook his head. "No."

Araminta busied herself with gathering up his clothing. "The police found a bloodied gardener's glove near the body."

"They suspect Yancy?"

Araminta grunted. "Suspect, yes. Have proof he is Shirley's killer? No. And I'm not so sure myself. There has been far too much movement after dark in this house since the rest of the family came, including yourself."

Puzzled, Reggie asked, "What do you mean?"

Remembering her promise to not tell on Angela and Owen, Araminta instead mentioned the reason she had come out to the gardener's shed in the first place. "Stephanie didn't join us for supper tonight. Someone mentioned she was out late last night too.

That is why I'm here. I saw a light out here in the woods and thought it was her or Yancy. Instead, I find you."

There was a look on his face, barely discernable in the low light, but Araminta saw it, just the same. "You have something to tell me? You saw something, didn't you?"

"Aunt Minty, Stephanie isn't the only one who has been out after dark, I'm afraid, but—I don't know if I should mention—"

Araminta straightened. "If you've seen someone, Reggie, I need to know. Whoever it was may well have been Shirley's killer!"

"I certainly hope not," Reginald muttered then shuddered as if with horror at the thought. "It would be quite terrible for her to be exonerated as a suspect in one possible murder, only to be embroiled in another."

Quick-witted as she was, Araminta knew exactly who her grandnephew was talking about. "Daisy? You saw your stepmother out after dark last night?"

Reggie shuffled his feet and hung his head, but he also nodded. "I saw her down at the solarium last night. I don't have my watch, but I'm pretty sure it was before midnight. Araminta, if Daisy killed Shirley…"

"Poppycock. She did no such thing," Araminta insisted immediately then wondered exactly when Shirley had been killed. She thought she'd heard the police mention the wee hours of the morning, but surely Daisy wouldn't have lain in wait since ten o'clock. "She had no motive, and besides, murder just isn't something I believe your stepmother could do."

Reggie nodded. "I don't believe she'd be capable either. Detective Hershey might, however, and I don't think she could handle suspicion being cast upon her again, but if they should find *me* here and ask that question…"

"Which is precisely why they aren't going to find you here, young man. You are to gather your belongings and come up to the house, as a proper Moorecliff heir should do." Handing him the clothing she had collected, Araminta said, "Skulking about here in the darkness instead of joining the loving comfort of your family inside would lead to naught but suspicion."

"But what about Daisy, Aunt Minty? She's going to be upset that I'm here."

Araminta needed a moment to consider. Finally, she said, "You will come inside and fess up to your stepmother. She will be disappointed, of course, but she will understand your wanting to be at your father's memorial."

"Maybe we shouldn't mention that I saw her… even to her."

Araminta shook her head. She admired how Reggie wanted to cover for his stepmother, but in her experience, it never worked out well. "It's good that you mentioned it. Now we have the opportunity to get ahead of it."

"What do you plan to do?" he asked.

Araminta turned and motioned for him to follow her from the shed. "I will find out why she was in the solarium last night before someone else who may have seen her there starts whispering and sowing seeds of doubt that she's responsible for Shirley's murder."

CHAPTER ELEVEN

*D*aisy was disappointed to learn Reginald had left the retreat, but she was still happy to see him. "But why are you both here in the middle of the night? Especially you, Araminta. I would have thought you'd be soundly sleeping."

"I was up thinking about the investigation." There was no casual way to broach the next topic, so Araminta went with her usual—blunt and outright. "Reginald saw you in the solarium late last night. Why were you there?"

"Well, let me see… I was in the solarium for a bit, helping Mary and Trinity with the food from the caterers, then I came back here to wait for…" Understanding dawned. She gasped, and her eyes went wide. "Oh, please! The sheer audacity! Are you thinking it, too, Reginald? Tell me you don't think I am Shirley's killer!"

"Of course we don't think you are," Reggie hurried to assure her. "We just want to know why you were there and who you were with at that hour. Daisy, you could have been in danger. There was a killer about!"

Daisy's eyes welled with emotion. Araminta knew how much it meant to her that Archie's children accepted her and cared for her as family. She was touched that Reggie genuinely seemed to care about her.

Araminta was touched, too, but it didn't really explain why Daisy was there late into the night. Trinity and Mary would have already gone home after dark, and Araminta knew they'd set up the solarium earlier in the day.

"I know you spent the day setting the solarium up, but Reggie saw you there late at night. Why?"

Daisy looked put out at the question. "What are you insinuating, Araminta?"

"Nothing, dear, I just wanted to know what you were doing so we can make sure it is explained properly." Why was Daisy acting so incredulous at the question? Araminta had seen her meeting with someone mysterious in the garden before, and she'd had a good reason. Could there be good reason for a second meeting?

Daisy looked away, her lips pursed. "I wasn't there…. oh, wait! The cake! I was there because of the cake."

Her shoulders slumped as she explained further. "I wanted to surprise everyone with a beautiful replica of Moorecliff Motors's most-famous car, so I had the bakery deliver it in secrecy. I scheduled the delivery for ten o'clock, because I knew everyone would be in bed by then."

So that explained why Araminta didn't remember the cake. Truth be told, she felt a little relieved that she wasn't forgetting things. No one had been allowed near the solarium, so if the cake had been delivered at night, Araminta would have had occasion to see it only when she discovered the body, and at that time, she'd been a bit distracted. Araminta looked at Reginald for verification of the timing.

"As I said before, I don't have my watch. I just know it had been dark for a while when I saw her, so I suppose it could have been around ten."

"You may verify it with the bakery, if you don't believe me," Daisy said, affronted by their doubt.

"We believe you, Daisy," Reginald assured her

again, then he gave her a quick hug for good measure. The cats must have believed her as well, because they rubbed their cheeks on her ankles and purred to show their support. "But if anyone else saw you creeping around out there in the dark like I did, there could be trouble. That's why Aunt Minty and I came to you. We wanted to ask what was up in case someone else brings it up. In case the police question you."

Daisy looked at Araminta, her gaze questioning. She tilted her head toward Reggie. "How did you know Reggie was here?"

"I was pacing in the sitting room, and I saw a light out at the edge of the woods through my window."

"But weren't you sleeping? Did someone or something wake you up?"

Now it was Araminta's time to confess. "I couldn't sleep. I was watching for Stephanie."

Daisy frowned. "She isn't home? But it's one a.m."

"She didn't join us for dinner, Daisy. If she were home, would she not have come down? I think she's out again, just like last night, when she sneaked in through the back door by the kitchen."

"Sneaked in?" Daisy's eyes widened. "You saw her?"

Araminta shook her head. "No, but someone did, and with a murderer obviously on the grounds, you know that could mean trouble for her."

"No!" Daisy exclaimed, her tone adamant. "Stephanie did not kill Shirley. Why would she?"

Daisy began to pace. "Why would she have done so? She barely knows Shirley, and she has only just returned to the family. For anyone to suspect Stephanie of having killed her gossipy old aunt would be ludicrous, because of us all, Steph would have the least reason to."

She turned to Araminta. "I know you've thought of a plan, Araminta. Tell us—what can we do? I won't let this happen, not when Stephanie is finally opening up to me. Please, say there is something we can do to prevent her from becoming an object of suspicion."

Araminta hated to upset Daisy again, but she knew the evidence found thus far could be used to present a case against Stephanie. If chance and circumstance presented itself, Olive would definitely tell the police what she knew about Angie and Owen. And then Angie, thinking Araminta had lied and betrayed her confidence would, in turn, feel obligated to tell what she knew about Stephanie's late-night entrance.

If events did, indeed, happen that way, Araminta knew there would be nothing she or Daisy could do to save the girl, other than hope she had an airtight alibi for where she was during the time of Shirley's murder.

Daisy, overcome with emotion, had tears pooled in her eyes again. And poor Reggie. It was clear he, too, was concerned for his sister, but what could they possibly do?

"Don't worry. All will be well," Araminta quickly reassured them. "I won't let this fall on Stephanie."

Daisy looked doubtful. "You have a plan?"

Araminta straightened, pretending for all she was worth that she had everything well in hand, though she hadn't a clue what to do at this point. Not that she would admit as much. Instead, she steeled her spine with a bravado she really didn't have and said, "I will simply find the real killer before anyone has a chance to accuse Stephanie."

CHAPTER TWELVE

The next morning, Araminta woke to the cheery sound of humming and whistling in the garden drifting in through her open window. She slipped on a robe and her slippers and went to the window to see who was so jovial this early in the morning. It was Yancy. He was back.

Oddly enough, he had simply resumed his normal duties in the garden with neither fuss nor warning of his return. "Well, would you look at that," Araminta told the cats. "It's as if he hasn't a clue about what went on here at Moorecliff Manor yesterday."

Araminta hurried to her wardrobe to dress. Since he'd returned, she needed to ask him a few questions before Detective Hershey found out and started to interrogate him. It felt strange to know she could soon be facing a murderer. But if he had recently committed such a heinous crime, you wouldn't know it by his demeanor. No, he seemed much too jovial and lively this morning for someone who had recently killed an ex-lover.

Or perhaps that was why he was in a good mood in the first place?

Araminta's hand paused in the act of pulling a brush through her silver hair as she considered the possibility, then she continued to quickly groom her hair with a renewed determination. If she wanted to know where Yancy had been last night, there was only one way to find out: she would have to ask him.

Araminta rushed through her morning routine, eager to get to Yancy before anyone else. Unfortunately, she ran smack-dab into Prudence Abernathy on the way out.

"Oh, morning, Pru." Araminta didn't want to be rude, but she was in a hurry. Why was Pru hovering in the main foyer anyway? "I trust you slept well."

Pru scowled. "Not so much. Laid awake all night, listening for mice."

"Did you hear any?" Araminta edged toward

the kitchen, where she intended to exit through the door closest to where she'd seen Yancy.

Pru pursed her lips and didn't look very happy about her answer. "No."

"See, there's no mouse infestation here. Perhaps that was some other noise you heard or just one mouse who the cats have chased out."

Pru's pursed lips tightened even further. "I doubt it. Once you get infested, you can't easily get rid of them."

"Ms. Abernathy, there you are." Harold came down the hall with a white package the size of a breadbox and handed it to Prudence.

Araminta's curiously was roused. What could Pru possibly be getting in a package? And why? But she didn't have time to investigate. It was probably a new batch of grouch pills or maybe a book on how to complain more.

Prudence's attention was now focused on Harold and the box, so Araminta took the opportunity to sneak away and rushed outside to find Yancy.

By the time she made her way out to the garden, she was near out of breath and the police were already there.

Who had called them to notify the detective of

Yancy's arrival? Had it been Prudence? She was certainly up and lurking about. Who else was out at this time of the morning? Slowing her pace, Araminta scanned the grounds. A flash of sunlight caught her attention. She turned and squinted into the morning sun to find what had caused it.

Olive was there, but Araminta hardly thought she would have called the inspector. Olive was far too busy preening into her folding compact hand mirror, which she held close to her face as she tucked stray pieces of gray hair back into her bun, her bejeweled right hand deftly pulling them back and tucking them inside.

Araminta scoffed. Silly woman. One would think she believed she was forty years younger, the way she checked herself. Like a schoolgirl preparing to meet a suitor. A thought struck Araminta. Was Olive attracted to young Hershey? Or perhaps she'd expected Jacob Hershey to accompany his young nephew.

Jacob was closer to Olive's age. The thought of Olive with Jacob made Araminta feel strange, but she had no idea why. Perhaps a woman would soften his sour demeanor, and that would be a good thing as far as she was concerned.

Rather than attract attention herself, Araminta

chose stealth and made for the cover of shadow and shade, skirting the side of the house instead of treading across the main stretch of lawn to the wide patch of newly planted shrubbery and flowers. The specially chosen vegetation was lovely, positioned to surround a statue model of the most famous car ever built by Moorecliff Motors.

Daisy had affectionately called the area the Archibald Moorecliff Family Commemorative Garden, but right now, there was no commemorating going on. Instead, Yancy was standing on the gravel path near the statue in the middle of it all, speaking in low tones with Detective Hershey. Araminta sidled closer to better hear what they were saying.

"And you are the Moorecliff's gardener, correct?"

"Yes, sir. Name's Yancy. Is there something I can help you with?"

"I just have a few questions for you, if you don't mind," Hershey said. "Ms. Moorecliff said you'd been given the day off when I was here yesterday. Can you tell me where you were?"

Yancy nodded then shuffled his feet a bit. Araminta thought he might even be blushing. "I was on Day Street, sir."

Hershey nodded. "Day Street. Lovely area. Nice grounds too. Were you there all day? Or did you leave for a time? And might I ask what you were doing there?"

Yancy shuffled his feet again. "I would rather not, sir. It's kind of private, if you don't mind."

"I gathered that when Ms. Moorecliff mentioned you'd asked for the day off but hadn't said why. Perhaps you would like to explain now?"

When Yancy said nothing, Hershey prompted him again. "Day Street. Where you were yesterday. It's kind of important. What were you doing there? How long did you stay? Is there anyone who can vouch for your presence there?"

Yancy's expression clouded, and in that instant, it became painfully obvious to Araminta that Yancy didn't know yet about Shirley's murder.

When the detective merely held his silence, Yancy gave in with a sigh. "I was helping to build a playground for underprivileged kids, but I don't understand why that would be relevant to your presence here. Is there something going on I'm not aware of?"

His head cocked to one side, Hershey peered up at him. "There has, actually. I'm afraid there has been a murder. Perhaps you are acquainted with the deceased? Her name is Ms. Shirley Moorecliff."

Yancy blanched. "S-Sh-Shirley? She's dead?"

Hershey nodded and showed him a glove. Araminta recognized it as a match to the bloodied one they'd found near Shirley's body yesterday. "Is this your glove? You did say you work here in the garden, right?"

"No, sir. I mean, yes, I work in the gardens, but that is not my glove, sir. That one belongs to Miss Stephanie. She loves the garden—something I think she has realized only recently. She's been puttering around out here with me since she returned to the family after… after Master Archie's death… and it seems to occupy all her time."

When the man seemed hesitant to accept what he'd said as the truth, Yancy placed the glove over his large right hand aligning the thumb and fingers, which were a good half inch larger than the glove. "See? This one would never work for me. It is far too small. As I said, it belongs to Miss Stephanie."

"This is not good," Arun said as he watched Yancy illustrate the small size of the glove compared to his large hands.

"I don't think our dear Yancy realizes he has just put a bull's-eye on Steph's back," Sasha replied.

"Yes, but I don't think Hershey will jump to arrest her. Those two are googly-eyed over each other."

Sasha hissed in disgust. "Humans are so strange. Still, he is bound to follow up because he's quite diligent at his job."

Arun flicked his tail. "I agree. Now I regret leading them to the glove."

Sasha's whiskers twitched as she mulled that over. "We couldn't withhold evidence, and I'm sure they would have found it eventually. We know Stephanie didn't kill Shirley, so we will simply find the evidence that proves who the killer is and lead the humans in that direction."

Arun thought that was a good idea. "Who do you think the killer is?"

Sasha started toward the house, and he followed. "Well, we know Angie and Owen have something to hide."

"True, but there are many others that also have something to hide. This family is full of secrets."

"That's why we should sniff around in the guest's rooms. You never know what you might find. Like the note in Shirley's drapes."

"Hopefully, everyone will be up and about by now and no humans will see us, though it doesn't much matter if they do, because no one ever suspects our true mission." Arun was always amazed by how the humans thought cats did nothing but laze around and play all day. Whenever they were seen in a room they weren't supposed to be in, the humans never suspected they might actually be investigating. Of course, the cats used that to their advantage.

They jumped in through the cat door in the kitchen and detoured to inspect their stainless-steel bowls in the butler's pantry for any treats Mary might have put in. They were in luck—a small morsel of chicken rested in each bowl.

After polishing off the chicken, they made their way to the guest rooms, but their hopes of not running into any of the guests were dashed when they got to the top of the second floor and saw Olive standing in the vestibule in the landing at the top of the grand stairs, with her back to them.

"What is she doing?"

"Not sure. Perhaps looking out the window? I

saw her in the garden out there not long ago. Maybe she lost something out there and is trying to see it from above."

Arun lightened his step even further so as not to disturb her. The cats were light on their feet as it was, and since her back was to them, they could sneak by without notice.

Just as they passed Olive, a door clicked open, and their attention was drawn down the hall to Prudence, who was backing carefully out of a room.

Olive whirled around. Pru must have had good hearing—maybe too good, if she thought she heard mice in the house—and she spun around as well, gasping when she saw Olive.

"Oh! Morning," Pru said.

Olive nodded. "Morning."

"I was just, umm… getting ready for breakfast."

Olive straightened her blouse. "Me too."

Pru's eyes flicked from Olive to the window. "Right then. Shall we go together?"

They both seemed reluctant and started down the stairs. When Olive made a move toward them, though, Pru fell into step beside her.

"Odd behavior, not that it's unusual for Moore-cliffs to behave oddly," Arun said as they watched the two ladies descend the stairs.

"Indeed. But we have bigger fish to fry." Sasha turned down the hall then lifted her nose in the air and sniffed, her whiskers twitching. "Do you smell that?"

Arun sniffed. Sasha had a much better sense of smell, but he didn't like to let on about that. There was no need for her to get a big head about being better at something than he was. "Yes, very odd. Where is that coming from?"

Sasha was already homing in, making her way to a solid oak door. She pushed her nose to the sliver of a gap at the bottom.

Arun did the same, the pungent smell assaulting his senses. "Is it cheddar?"

Sasha took another good sniff. "No, I think maybe camembert."

Arun wasn't so sure. He turned the scent over in his mind, matching it with previous scents. "I think it's gouda."

"Well, any cheese is good, eh? But what is it doing in the closet?"

Arun pawed at the door, but it didn't budge. "Who knows? This door opens out, and we can't pry it open. Remember, we tried that before when the Sanderson twins were here and hid tuna sandwiches they didn't want to eat in their sweater pockets and then hung their sweaters in the hall closet?"

Sasha's whiskers twitched at the memory. "Yes! Trinity was quite upset when she made that discovery after they left."

"It was very smelly."

Sasha turned her attention back to the hallway. "Look, the door to Owen's room is open. Shall we peek inside? I think I saw him downstairs, so we'll have some time to explore."

CHAPTER THIRTEEN

Araminta ran into Daisy and Reggie in the kitchen. Reggie had made a ham-and-cheese sandwich but was having a hard time finding a knife to cut it with. One thing about her nephew —he liked to fend for himself and wasn't some spoiled kid who demanded the staff do everything for him. He also liked his sandwiches cut on the diagonal.

"Aunty Araminta, have you seen the serrated knives?" Reggie opened a drawer.

Araminta glanced at the butcher block holder where Mary kept the carving knives. It was empty.

"Just what do you think you're doing, Master Reggie?" Mary rushed over to Reggie and pulled the plate away, inspecting the sandwich as if to see if it was as good as one of hers. "It's my place to make the food. You need to stop being so independent."

Mary looked put out, as if hurt that Reggie hadn't asked her.

"I didn't want to bother you, but if you want to help, you could cut it for me," Reggie said.

Mary took a butter knife out of a drawer. "Have to use this. The police took all the knives." Mary lined the knife up against the sandwich, stooping until it was eye-level and then squinting one eyed shut as if cutting the sandwich with precision were of utmost importance. "They think one of the knives might be the murder weapon."

Daisy gasped. "One of our knives?"

Of course, it made perfect sense. Where else would the killer get a knife? Plus, the kitchen was near the conservatory. Araminta's stomach tightened as she remembered Angie's revelation about Stephanie sneaking through the kitchen door the night of the murder.

Mary cut the sandwich with a flourish and pushed it toward Reggie. "There now. I wish you people would let me do the job and stop lurking in the kitchen at all hours of the night."

"Lurking? Who has been lurking in the

kitchen?" Araminta hoped Mary didn't say it was Stephanie.

"That horrid Prudence Abernathy," Mary said, then her eyes got wide. She clapped her hand over her mouth and turned to Daisy. "Sorry, didn't mean to overstep."

"No problem," Daisy assured her. "She *is* horrid. What was she doing in here?"

"She was rummaging around in the butler's pantry. Said she needed a snack."

"Near the knives?" Araminta hoped.

"Not when I saw her, but she could have been there before I ran into her."

"Probably looking for mice." Reggie bit into his sandwich.

Araminta watched him chew as her mind swirled. Was Prudence really looking for a snack? What reason would she have to kill Shirley?

Her thoughts were interrupted by the kitchen door swinging open. In stepped Stephanie. She stopped short, clearly surprised to see them all gathered there. Her gaze stopped at Reggie, and her face broke into a smile. "Reg! What are you doing here?"

They hugged. "I really couldn't stay away from

Dad's memorial. I'm sorry to disappoint everyone, but I snuck away from the retreat."

"That's not a disappointment," Daisy said. "We're happy to see you."

"We are. It's great having you here. Did you just get in?" Stephanie asked.

"Something like that."

Apparently, Reggie didn't want to get into the whole story about how he'd been hiding in the gardener's shed. Araminta would keep his secret, and she was sure Daisy would too. They had bigger problems.

"Steph, we missed you at dinner last night," Araminta said, trying to sound as cheerful as possible. She didn't want Stephanie to think she was accusing her of anything, but she needed to find out where the girl had been. Hopefully, she hadn't been in the solarium, killing Shirley.

Stephanie looked guilty, her gaze flicking from Araminta to Daisy. "I'm sorry. I didn't realize anyone would miss me. There are so many Moorecliffs, and I'm afraid I was tired and Moorecliffed-out."

"Tired?" Araminta asked. "Is that why you've taken to sneaking in through the kitchen rather than enter the house like the rest of the family, through the front door?"

"Well, I wouldn't exactly call it sneaking. I was out in the garden pruning the azaleas, and this is the closest door."

"Yes, just now, but what about the night before last?"

Stephanie's gaze narrowed, and she started to look guilty. "What about it?"

"Someone said they saw you sneaking in through this very door in the wee hours of the morning."

Stephanie sighed. "I was at a party with friends and didn't want to run into anyone in the front hall."

Daisy walked over and hugged her. "Steph, you know I don't mind if you go off with your friends. But why sneak out? Why could you not just tell us?"

Stephanie's gaze was cast downward. "You know how people in this family talk. I'm sure some, like Aunt Shirley, would think it was disrespectful, and I just didn't want to deal with her nastiness."

Araminta felt a bit relieved that Stephanie had mentioned Shirley so casually. She must not know about the murder. Not that Araminta had suspected her niece, but one never knew. Araminta noticed another thing too. The relationship between Daisy and Stephanie had always been very strained, but not for lack of trying on Daisy's part. This time, though, Steph did not seem as stiff when Daisy hugged her, and she almost hugged her stepmother back.

Araminta figured she'd better warn the girl. "Steph, Detective Hershey is here. He will want to question you soon."

"Me? But why?"

"I guess you haven't talked to anyone from the family lately." Reggie polished off the last of the sandwich.

Stephanie frowned. "I try not to. I've been in my room and then out in the garden. What's going on?"

"Shirley was murdered." Might as well just blurt it out.

Stephanie gasped. "Aunty Shirley? The one who knew everyone's dirty business?"

"That's the one," Daisy said.

"Oh." Stephanie looked shocked, but not terribly sad. She hadn't been that close to Shirley, and Shirley hadn't been exactly likeable. "Who did it?"

"We don't know. That's why Hershey is investigating."

"Why would he want to talk to me, though? I don't know anything about it."

"You've been helping Yancy in the garden, right?" Araminta asked.

She nodded. "I find the effort therapeutic."

After a moment, Stephanie realized what Araminta was getting at. Her voice lowered to barely more than a whisper, she asked, "They think Yancy killed her? But why would he do such a thing? What proof do they have?"

"There was a bloody glove, and it turns out Yancy and Shirley were having a fling."

"Well, that's no reason to kill her, and besides, we all know Yancy wouldn't hurt a fly," Stephanie said.

Daisy nodded. "I put my money on blackmail. Aunt Shirley was always trying to profit from what she knows, and maybe someone got sick of it."

"And there *was* a note to meet her in the solarium," Araminta added.

Stephanie frowned. "So it was premeditated."

Araminta raised a brow. Apparently, her young niece had been hanging around with Ivan Hershey enough to pick up on some of the police terminology. "Which indicates it wasn't a crime of passion like it might have been if she and Yancy got into an argument."

Stephanie nodded. "Probably one of the relatives that was being blackmailed, then. I'll seek out Hershey and vouch for Yancy."

"That would be good," Araminta said. "But there's something else you might want to be aware of before you do."

Steph had been on her way to the door, but then she turned to face Araminta. "What?"

"The bloody glove was yours."

CHAPTER FOURTEEN

Araminta was at her wits' end. The police had questioned Yancy and were now combing the grounds in search of the murder weapon. Apparently, they hadn't located it among the knives they took from the kitchen. Detective Hershey was overseeing the process and had commanded his team to leave no leaf unturned.

While they were busy, Araminta decided it would be a good time to slip upstairs to search the guests' rooms for clues—before the whispers started and fingers were pointed at Stephanie.

Araminta didn't really like snooping in people's things, but she had to do it for Stephanie. She searched Cousin Charlotte's room, her grandnephew Terrence's room, and her second cousin Velda's room, but she came up empty.

It was in Owen's room that she hit pay dirt in the old oak rolltop desk that was once her grandfather's. She had fond memories of Gramps sitting there, writing with his fountain pen. The blots of ink that had spattered from it were still visible on the worn surface of the desk.

The cats had followed her in and then proceeded to jump up onto the top of the desk and meander around, flicking their tails and meowing.

"Yes, it is a lovely piece, isn't it?" Araminta said to the cats as she ran her hands along the surface and opened the door to one of the cubbies just like she'd done many times as a little girl.

"Meow!" Arun pawed at the narrow drawers in the center, and she wondered if they still stuck like they had when she was little. She opened one, and that was where she found the letters.

There were five of them, written from Angie to Owen. Though Araminta tried not to read the contents of the letters, she was certain Angela would not want her husband to see them. But she had to take a little peek, just to see if the writing matched the note she'd found in Shirley's room. The penmanship was similar—fine with open, scrolling letters—but she couldn't be sure the handwriting matched without a side-by-side comparison. Plus, she had given the other note to Hershey—something she could not do with these. Not if she wanted to continue to protect Angela and Owen's secret.

"Meow." Arun rubbed his cheek against the edge of the letters.

"Yes, indeed. This is a bit of a pickle. How can I do a comparison? I promised Angie I wouldn't let on about her secret, so I can't show the letters to anyone, and there is no way for me to get the other letter from Hershey." Could she somehow get a photo of the other letter? Perhaps Stephanie could help? But it must be in evidence by now, and even though she suspected Ivan Hershey was a bit enamored with Steph, she was certain he wouldn't let her plunder about in the evidence room.

Before she could think further, the cats suddenly jumped down from the desk and rushed back and forth between Araminta and the door, their tails held high in the air.

A board creaked in the hall. Someone was coming!

She shoved the letters back into the drawer. She couldn't get caught in Owen's room and have to answer a lot of questions. Luckily, she had the perfect excuse. She rushed over to the doorway.

"Now go on, you scamps. You know you aren't supposed to be in the guests' rooms!" she said very loudly as she backed out of the room, making shooing gestures with her arms as if she'd only been in the room to shoo the cats out.

She turned, surprised to find Olive standing there. "Oh, sorry, Olive. Didn't see you there. Darned cats are so mischievous!"

Olive's gaze flicked from the cats to Owen's open door. She stepped closer to Araminta. "That's Owen's room. Were you investigating? I was right, wasn't I?"

Araminta supposed it wasn't going back on her word to Angie if she confirmed Olive's suspicions about the affair. Olive had been the one to tell her in the first place. "Yes, you were."

"Did one of them kill Shirley?" Olive's lower lip trembled. She looked like she was about to burst into tears, and Araminta hastened to assure her she wasn't sure. "There's no evidence right now to confirm that." The last thing she needed was to have Olive yell out accusations against Angie and Owen, especially if they didn't have anything to do with Shirley's death. She still wasn't sure about that, but if they were innocent, it wouldn't be right to let on about the affair.

"But you suspect them?" Olive persisted.

"Among others." Araminta didn't want to encourage Olive. Best to make a quick getaway. "I really must run. I have an important call to make."

"Of course." Olive reluctantly moved out of the way. "But you'll let me know when you find anything out?"

"You'll be the first to know!"

Araminta rushed down the stairs. She actually did have an important call to make, one she dreaded and would never even consider making unless it was a last resort. But she was out of ideas and was worried about the evidence that seemed to point toward Stephanie.

She closeted herself in Daisy's office. This was only the second room in the manor still sporting a phone connected via landline. She dialed the one number she'd never thought she would dial, put the receiver to her ear, and waited.

After several rings, she heard the line connect then a bit of a grumble before the person she'd rung finally spoke. "You've reached the Hershey residence. May I ask with whom I am speaking?"

"Jacob Hershey, you know who I am. I know you've got your caller ID on."

Araminta fidgeted for a moment with the receiver cord then swallowed back her pride. Stephanie's future depended on whether or not Jacob could help her piece things together, so she pushed her feelings for Jacob aside and got down to brass tacks. "You're the last man I wanted to call on, but I find myself in a time-sensitive twisted pickle. Do you think, for just a moment perhaps, that you could put your animosity toward me aside and lend an ear to my dilemma… and maybe give a bit of advice?"

"Ah, Araminta. How lovely of you to call. Dare I trust my ears? Could swear I heard you say you really need my help."

A roll of her eyes said she noted the way he'd changed up what she had actually said, but for now, she decided to ignore it. She told him everything she knew about the situation at hand: the murder with no weapon, the gloves, the note, and the letters. She even told him about Daisy and Reginald and Stephanie.

Finally, once she had wound down to give him time to process his thoughts, Araminta spoke into the phone. "Well? Are you still there? Or, more importantly, what am I missing?"

"Of course I am here, Araminta. Where would I go? I'm thinking about the notes and letters. Penmanship is all good and fine, but did you notice any particular slant to the letters?"

Araminta had forgotten about that part: right-handed people tended to slant their letters in one direction, while left-handed folks leaned them in the other. "No, I didn't. And I gave the first note to your grandson, so I cannot compare them. But if memory serves, both bits of writing slanted to the right. Which would mean the killer could be right-handed."

"There is that," Jacob agreed. "Still just circumstantial. Sounds like a mess, to be sure, and I can't think of any way you can look at the first letter. You'll have to find another clue. How will you protect Stephanie?"

Araminta frowned. "Well, I had hoped you'd be more help, Jacob. That poor girl, she's so young, and if Ivan arrests her—"

Jacob interrupted, "Don't be so quick to write off the girl's mettle, Minta, darling. She is Archie's daughter, after all. A true Moorecliff if ever I've seen one. Reminds me of yourself, actually, from back in the day."

"Heaven help us if you're crushing on old memories, Jacob," Araminta grouched, although she could feel the heat of a pleasant blush warming her cheeks.

Jacob laughed. "Don't go fishing for compliments, Minta. My point was that this particular branch of the Moorecliff family tends to be bright, if a bit soft. But you of all people should know by now the apple never falls far from the tree."

CHAPTER FIFTEEN

Instead of following Araminta downstairs, the cats had remained on the second floor. Lingering outside the cheese-scented closet, they watched as Angie and Owen snuck back into his room.

Both cats crept toward the door, their ears angled to catch any whispers of conversation.

A voice sounded from the other side of the door. "We have to be careful, Angela. If this gets out…"

The fur on Arun's neck stood on end. It was Owen. He was warning Angie about something, but what?

Two seconds later, he heard Owen say, "The

police are asking a lot of questions. If they find the letters you wrote, they will know everything."

Eyes narrowed, Arun glanced at Sasha. Everything? Was he merely referring to the affair, or did "everything" include murder?

"We will be fine," a voice Arun recognized as Angie's said. "Look, I have them all now. Don't worry. No one knows. No one will find out."

He must have indicated that he didn't feel as confident of their escaping unscathed as Angela, because she followed her reassurances with "But you are right. We must destroy all the evidence." Her tone was pouty.

Evidence?

Was she disappointed because he wanted her to get rid of the murder weapon? Absurd. What murderer in their right mind didn't want to get rid of evidence? Arun nudged closer to the door. If the murder weapon was in Owen's room, he needed to see it.

There was another long stretch of silence, then Angie opened the door and stepped out into the hallway so quickly, Arun had to sprint to the side to keep from being mangled by her glossy red heels. She had something in her hand, but he'd had to run away so quickly, he hadn't seen what it was.

Hurrying to Sasha now, he hunkered down beside her and watched in silence as Angela Moore-cliff walked to the end of the hall and glanced both ways to be sure no one was about to see what she was doing. At first, he thought she might be about to open the hall window that was in a vestibule opposite the grand stairway, but then she slid open a hidden panel in the wall.

Memories rushed in of a small box. Darkness. Sailing downward, only to be pushed back inside it, and then black until he reached the top again. Arun felt nauseated. Sasha nudged him with her nose in commiseration, but she didn't take her eyes off Angela.

Papers. Arun realized Angela was holding a handful of papers the same instant she tossed them into the void of darkness she had revealed, and then she slid the panel closed again. Only papers. Not the murder weapon.

"It's the old dumbwaiter. David showed it to me one time when we were first married," she explained to Owen, who had stepped out into the hallway, presumably to keep watch in case someone came upstairs while Angela was dumping the evidence.

Owen nodded. "I remember it from when I was

a kid. No one uses it anymore. I haven't even thought of it in years."

"That's what makes it the perfect hiding place for the letters. I know we should destroy them, but I don't have the heart. After the investigation is over, we can retrieve them."

Owen frowned. Arun thought he was about to protest, but Angie rose up on her toes and pressed a quick, silencing kiss on his lips. She reached up to soothe his brow with her fingers, almost as if she thought she could wipe away his fierce look of skepticism. His brow smoothed, and she smiled. "No one will think to look in there, I promise. Our secret is safe, my darling."

Forced to rely on her promise that all would be well, Owen reluctantly pulled the door closed behind him and then followed Angie downstairs.

Sasha looked at Arun. She knew he was uncomfortable, because she knew what the Moorecliff cousins had used the dumbwaiter for in times long past—a device for feline torture neither she nor he would ever forget. But rather than bring up more bad memories, she chose to focus on the present. Nudging him again, she asked, "What now?"

Arun stretched out beneath the panel Angie had opened, then he curled up in a ball, his chin resting on outstretched paws much the same as he had earlier in front of Owen's door. If one of them was the killer, those papers might be the thing that could help match the handwriting to the note they'd found in Shirley's room. They could be important, but Arun wondered if Araminta would think so too. "Now we wait for Araminta."

CHAPTER SIXTEEN

*A*fter ending her call with Jacob, Araminta decided to run back upstairs to have another look at the letters Angie had written to Owen. Jacob's comment about the slant of the letters had her thinking. She might not be able to look at the letter she found in Shirley's room, but she could at least try to ascertain if Angie was left- or right-handed. Maybe she would be able to sweet-talk Ivan Hershey into telling her if the stab wounds indicated which hand the killer used.

She had barely rounded the corner toward Owen's room at the top when she was waylaid by the cats.

Sasha ran to the landing area by the window then waited for Araminta to follow. Arun walked a few steps ahead of her, but then he stopped and stretched up onto the mahogany-paneled section of the wall, putting both front feet as high up as he could reach.

He began to knead the wall with his claws. Sasha meowed so loud, Araminta knelt and scooped her up into her arms for a quick pet.

"Quiet now, you two. Stop that, Arun. You'll scratch the wood! I've spoken with Jacob, and he has given me little help, but I need another look at those letters Angela wrote."

Sasha didn't wait to be put down. Araminta was taken aback when the cat scrambled from her arms and rushed to Arun's side to join him in mauling the wall.

"None of that, now. Trinity will not like it if she has to cover up scratches in the paneling," Araminta scolded, then she drew up, her narrowed gaze focused on the wall the cats were currently using as a temporary scratching post. They were trying to tell her something. "Have you heard something in there?"

Yesterday, Prudence had sworn she'd heard mice in the walls, and now these two seemed determined to tear their way into them for some reason. But mice?

It'd seemed highly improbable when Pru mentioned it at the table… of all places… but if there were rodents scurrying around inside the walls, Araminta knew it was best they find out early rather than late.

But why would the cats be concerned about that when there was a murder investigation going on? Araminta stood back and studied the wall. The panels were polished to perfection, and the handle blended in seamlessly. The handle! She'd almost forgotten about the old dumbwaiter hidden discreetly behind the panel.

As a child, she had played in the hand-drawn elevator, along with her cousins and several of their friends. The old box was hand-worked with a rope-and-pulley system, which butlers and maids would use to move meal trays and laundry to the basement. Over the years, the staff at Moorecliff Manor had been reduced, and the family had become more self-sufficient. The dumbwaiter hadn't been used in decades.

There was a separate section in the back of it, if she correctly recalled how it was put together. Yes, there was. It was originally used to put a small block of ice to keep things chilled in the smaller compartment while it was on the way up to the family's rooms. She remembered she used to hide things in it.

Later, her nieces and nephews had played in it, too, and some of them were wont to put the cats inside the thing and send them up and down or tie it off halfway between floors, where they would leave it until someone missed the cats. Her brows drew downward. "Is that why you brought me here? Has someone been putting you two in this thing?"

No, that couldn't be it, Araminta decided. She would be surprised if it even still functioned. Sliding the panel aside, Araminta peered into the darkness. The first thing she noticed was that the box itself wasn't on this floor. The next thing was that the rope used to pull the thing up was missing. It had been frayed from use years ago; she wasn't surprised at all that it had finally broken. Reaching up, she turned the large cast-iron wheel that the rope used to be attached to.

Squeak, squeak, squeak.

Could the squeaking be what Prudence had heard? But the rope was broken, which meant the dumbwaiter didn't work, and therefore, no one would be pulling it up to produce the squeak. And it must have broken long ago, or surely someone would have heard it crash to the basement.

Unless… someone sent it down to the basement and then cut the rope on purpose so that no one would be able to bring it up.

Owen's room was on this floor—he or Angie could have easily done it.

Movement outside the window caught her eye. Yancy was in the garden, using a rake to clear some leaves that had fallen where they shouldn't. He was quietly going about his daily routine, blithely minding his own business. For someone who had just been a murder suspect, he seemed quite calm.

Araminta thought of his recently resumed relationship with Shirley—and perhaps some others if what Stephanie had said was correct. Had he killed Shirley? If he had, why? Nothing was amiss in the gardener's shed—other than the things that Reginald had brought in.

For the life of her, Araminta could not imagine the gentle soul that was Yancy raising a hand to another. How could this man possibly be guilty of murder? She found it hard to believe, but she knew Stephanie was not the one, despite the glove the police had found. But if it had been Yancy, why would he use Stephanie's glove? Knowing Steph, she had left it hanging around where anyone could have grabbed it.

Araminta continued to watch him rake back the leaves for a moment, his strong hands grabbing the handle of the rake and pulling.

His hands! An image of him holding the glove up against his right hand to illustrate bubbled up.

Wait! He'd matched the glove to his right hand, laying it on top, which meant the glove was right-handed. That glove wasn't the bloodied glove though, that was the match. So the bloodied glove was the left glove! With that bit of information, Araminta didn't need Ivan Hershey to tell her that the killer was left-handed!

Without waiting around or bothering to explain herself, Araminta whirled around and rushed down to the hall. She had to have a second look at those letters inside Owen's room.

CHAPTER SEVENTEEN

The letters were gone. They weren't in the desk where she'd found them originally, and she'd even searched the room, thinking Owen or Angie might have moved them. "Where have they put them? The letters have to be here somewhere!"

"Meow!" Arun trotted from Araminta to the door, glancing at her over his shoulder as if to agree she would find nothing in the room and should leave.

Loathe to admit defeat, Araminta took one last look around and followed him out.

"Well, if you two have any other ideas, I'm all ears," Araminta said to the cats, who had trotted into the hallway and were pacing in front of the closet door.

Hadn't Angie said something about seeing Prudence in front of the door?

Araminta tried the knob. Locked.

"Hmm… that's odd. Why is this locked?"

Arun looked up wide-eyed, as if to indicate he had the same question. Sasha had trotted over to the dumbwaiter again and was pacing back and forth, tail straight up in the air.

"There's nothing in there, Sash. I have already checked…"

Araminta started and then paused. No, she hadn't checked. Not really. She had opened the panel and realized the dumbwaiter wasn't on this floor, but she hadn't looked down into the shaft…

"I'll need a light. It's very dark inside. But if there's aught to be found, rest assured, I shall find it," Araminta promised. After a quick trip to her own bedroom, where she collected the small penlight from her nightstand, Araminta again stood in front of the panel covering the opening for the dumbwaiter. She slid it open and leaned in with the light to have a look inside.

"I've found the letters!" she called back to the cats. "But they are inaccessible. The dumbwaiter is lodged in the shaft down near the basement. The papers are on top of it."

Meow!

Araminta withdrew from the entrance to the service elevator and snapped off the light then closed the panel. "I'll have to dislodge the box, but the only access is through the basement."

If she could get a look at the letters, she could determine if Angie was left-handed. If not, then she likely wasn't the killer. Of course, that didn't leave Owen out, but at least one suspect would be eliminated. She glanced at the closet and thought about Prudence. Was Prudence a leftie, and what did the closet have to do with anything? Maybe Angie had seen Prudence at the dumbwaiter and mistaken it for the closet?

Araminta turned her attention back to the dumbwaiter. With the police searching the house for the murder weapon, it made sense that Angie would get rid of the letters—even if they didn't mention the murder, the letters would expose their affair. No one would look in the dumbwaiter, and if they did, they certainly wouldn't look on top of it. That made Araminta wonder… had someone broken it on purpose so they could hide something on top or inside… like the murder weapon?

Araminta shined the light inside, this time looking for the rope. One end lay twisted beneath the tangle of letters Angela had dropped inside the shaft, but the other end… was cut.

The rope hadn't broken. It had been cut clean through! But why would Angela cut the rope to try and hide the letters? Peering intently at the severed end, she noticed something on the cording, and she didn't need to get closer to figure out what it was.

Blood. There was blood on the rope to the dumbwaiter. Was it blood from the knife that had killed Shirley?

Araminta blinked, trying to make sense of it all.

Whoever had knifed Shirley had probably done the deed in the solarium, then rushed upstairs to their room, but then realized they would need to dispose of the murder weapon and decided to hide it in the dumbwaiter.

So why cut the rope?

Anyone who remembered the dumbwaiter from their childhood, like she had, might have opened the thing and found the knife. Then it would only be a short time before the killer was exposed, so they'd cut the rope but held on to the carriage long enough to hide the knife inside it then sent it to the basement to collect and get rid of later.

Yes, Araminta decided. That must have been it. But the dumbwaiter had lodged in the shaft, making it impossible to collect the knife. Someone would have to try to jiggle the box down to the basement to get it open. And that would create a lot of noise.

There were never any mice in the manor. What there was, however, was a murderer!

CHAPTER EIGHTEEN

What person in their right mind went into a dark basement alone while looking for a murder weapon? None, Araminta belatedly realized. She was alone, and the only thing she had with her for protection was a tiny penlight and two Siamese cats. Perhaps she shouldn't have brushed off Trinity's offer to accompany her when she rushed past the girl in the kitchen.

Hesitant now, she wondered if she should go back and bring the police down with her. No. That would take too long, and the killer might hear them and get there first. Hopefully, they weren't already down there, and Araminta could check her theory about the knife and then call in the police. She didn't want to ruin her reputation by making an announcement that the murder weapon was here and drag everyone down, only to discover she was wrong. She'd learned her lesson long ago to double-check before alerting the authorities.

Araminta crept slowly into the basement, swinging her small light back and forth.

Her heart leapt when the beam of light fell on a figure crouched in the corner.

"Aha!" Araminta shouted even as her brow creased in confusion. This wasn't where the dumb-waiter was located. Had the killer already retrieved the knife and was now hiding it?

The figure spun around, shading their eyes from the light. "Araminta, what in the world are you doing?"

It was Prudence!

"Catching a killer." Araminta angled the light to the left so she could see the guilty look on Pru's face. Except Pru didn't look guilty; she looked confused.

The cats had trotted over to Prudence and were sniffing around at something behind her—ferreting out the murder weapon, no doubt.

"Killer? what are you talking about? Have you gone daft?" Prudence asked.

"I caught you red-handed trying to hide the

evidence. Now step aside and let me see." Araminta gestured with the flashlight.

She expected more of a fight, but Prudence simply gave her a funny look and then stepped to the side to reveal…

A mousetrap?

"What is that?" Araminta trained the light on the trap.

"Figures you don't know what it is. It's a mouse-trap." Prudence fisted her hands on her hips and looked disgusted. "Someone has to take steps to catch the mice in here instead of denying that they exist."

"Where did you get a mousetrap?" Araminta stepped closer. She could see a piece of Swiss cheese in the trap. The cats were circling it, their whiskers twitching as they looked at each other with knowing glances.

"I ordered it online and had it delivered here," Prudence said. "Do you think I'm too old to order stuff online? And then I simply got some cheese from the fridge. Your cook didn't seem too happy, but someone has to do something to get rid of these things."

"So that's what you're doing down here? Setting mousetraps?" Araminta asked.

"Actually, I was checking this one. That's why the lights are off. I don't want to scare any mice off, so I sneak up with my tiny penlight." Prudence took a small keychain flashlight out of her pocket and showed it to Araminta, then she reached over and flicked a switch on the wall.

The basement lighting consisted of dim bulbs that hung from the ceiling, casting circular beams of light below them. It was still pretty dim down there, but the bulbs were a lot better than the flashlight Araminta had been using. Now she realized how silly it was to use it when she could have just turned on the basement lights. Perhaps she'd been watching too many scary movies.

Araminta eyed the empty trap. "Have you caught any mice?"

Prudence looked disappointed. "No. Not here. Not in the closet. Not in the butler's pantry."

Araminta felt a little better that the manor really didn't have a mouse infestation, which reminded her of the real source of the squeaking. "What about the dumbwaiter?"

Prudence's eyes lit up. "The dumbwaiter! I had forgotten all about that. That's a good idea. I bet there will be some mice in there."

"Well now, hang on there." The last thing

Araminta needed was Prudence going to the dumbwaiter and finding Angie's letters. Her mention of it had served a purpose, though. Pru's eagerness to put a mousetrap in there indicated she wasn't the killer. Nor did she have anything hidden in there, as she would surely want to avoid Araminta exploring the dumbwaiter in that case.

"Did you put a trap in the hall closet near the bedrooms and lock it?" Araminta asked.

"Of course. That seems to be the direction where the most noise is coming from." Prudence produced a small skeleton key from her pocket. "These old skeleton keys work on all the doors. I didn't want that nosey maid removing the trap."

"Good thinking."

Prudence looked pleased at the compliment, then her expression turned suspicious. "What are *you* doing down here? You mentioned something about the killer?" Pru glanced around as if the killer could be lurking in the shadows.

Araminta waved her hand dismissively. "Never mind that. I was just talking to the cats. I was wondering if the cats had killed some mice down here." She didn't want Prudence in on her theory about the knife being in the dumbwaiter.

"Well, if you ask me, judging by the noise in the

walls, they have their work cut out for them." Prudence glanced down at the cats, who were now grooming themselves, and shook her head, then she started toward the stairs. "Now don't let them touch this trap. It's all set up, but if I want to put one in the dumbwaiter, I better get upstairs and order another one online."

Araminta let her go, relieved that she was leaving. Prudence wasn't the killer, but she still hadn't ruled out Angie.

"One suspect has been ruled out. Now to see if we can rule out another," Araminta whispered to the cats as she headed toward the dumbwaiter. She needed to get a look at those letters.

The dumbwaiter was in the dimmest corner of the basement. Spiderwebs and dust were everywhere, but Araminta soldiered on. The sooner she could figure out who the killer was, the better.

The old door opened easily enough, but she could see that the dumbwaiter itself was lodged a few feet up in the shaft. She could also see fresh scrapes in the metal and chips in the wood. Someone had been trying to pry it down.

"You always were too nosey for your own good."

Araminta had been too intent on the task to

notice the cats' warnings or see someone sneaking up behind her.

She whirled around to see Olive standing there, a look of rage on her face and a crowbar held high as if to strike Araminta with it. It didn't escape Araminta that the weapon was in her *left* hand.

CHAPTER NINETEEN

Images of Olive under the tree with her compact bubbled up. Darn! Araminta cursed herself for not realizing that she'd been holding it in her left hand, as one who was left-handed would do. But Olive had seemed so upset about Shirley's demise… would she really have killed her own sister? Araminta needed to buy some time, to get Olive talking.

The cats might have had a plan too—they were meowing and doing circle eights around Olive's ankles.

"Olive! What do you mean?"

Olive's gaze flicked to the dumbwaiter. "You know what I mean. You've been asking questions and investigating. Clearly, you think the dumbwaiter is of interest, and I suppose you've figured it all out."

There's was no point in trying to get away by pretending she didn't suspect Olive at this point. By the menacing look on Olive's face, she meant business, so Araminta simply said, "I did. I should have realized from the beginning, Olive, when you were so eager to spill family secrets. But then, the apple never does fall far from the tree, does it?"

"What is that supposed to mean?" Olive demanded.

Araminta shrugged. "Shirley was a bad apple, stooping to anything to get her way, and now it appears you've followed suit. And taken up some of her methods, such as trying to frame Angela and Owen for her murder and using Stephanie's gardening glove to throw things off track."

Olive's arm must have been getting tired. She lowered the crowbar a few inches, an evil smile spreading across her face. "There's no proof to tie me to it. Haven't you heard? The police cannot find a murder weapon."

"Not yet," Araminta agreed, slyly creeping closer to Olive. "But I suspect they will have a better idea once they piece things together."

Olive's eyes narrowed, and she stepped closer. Araminta shrank back, thinking she might strike.

The cats meowed in alarm.

Olive scowled at the cats. "Quiet, you two."

Araminta got ready to assume her karate stance, but instead of attacking her, Olive went to the dumbwaiter.

"I see you didn't make any progress getting this thing loose either," Olive said over her shoulder.

"I barely got a chance." Araminta watched as Olive got to work prying the side of the box away from the shaft.

With Olive's attention on freeing the dumbwaiter, Araminta could have taken the opportunity to run, but she didn't. Now that she had Olive in this crazed state, she could get a clear confession, and since Olive was doing all the work to free the murder weapon, why not let her?

"So, why did you do it? Was it Yancy?" Araminta had a pretty good idea now, but she wanted to hear it from Olive.

"He loved *me*," she said without pausing in her attempts to free the dumbwaiter. In fact, her attempts to loosen the box became more frantic. "*Me*. Not Shirley. Never Shirley."

Araminta noticed the dark flush staining Olive's

cheeks and realized she was likely furious and battling herself over the truth of the matter, though her version existed only in her imagination.

"I suppose you must have seen them together on the grounds? You realized they'd rekindled their old relationship."

Olive spun around to face Araminta, her expression full of fury. "They were talking about the future! Where they would go when Yancy retired, to live out the rest of their lives together." She shook her head then went back to work at the dumbwaiter. She seemed to have forgotten Araminta was still in the room.

Still not quite a confession and there was one thing still bothering Araminta.

"Is that how you knew about the special cake Daisy had made for the memorial? You were in the solarium that night after it was delivered," Araminta said. She needed Olive to pay attention—at least until she got a specific confession. With Olive focused on the events as they had happened, Araminta was sure she would get the truth out of her.

"What? I guess. I didn't much pay attention to the food."

But Araminta remembered she'd mentioned it when Prudence had noted all the food would go to waste. Then later on, when Daisy had confessed that she'd been in the solarium late, Araminta should have realized that Olive could have known about the cake only if she'd been in the solarium even later than Daisy.

"You knew that Shirley was using her knowledge of certain family members' secrets for her own personal gain and that she was having secret meetings to collect her payments, so you simply left a note in her room to meet in the solarium. You knew Shirley would show up to collect, didn't you? Then you went through the kitchen before making your way back to the solarium. That's where you got the knife."

A loud thump followed by a crash made Araminta jump reflexively, and Olive flinched too. She stepped back from the dumbwaiter portal for a second as a couple sheets of paper swooshed out with the dust when it landed. She waved at the dust, shooing it away from her face, then reached inside the separate section on the side of the dumbwaiter box that was used to keep food cold and took out the knife she'd used to murder her own sister before turning at last to face Araminta. "You're right, Araminta. You are always right. But this time, it won't do you any good, because you know too much, and now I have to kill you."

The cats went crazy meowing and clawing at Olive. Arun even jumped up and hung off her sleeve, his claws ripping into the cotton fabric.

She shook them off easily and then advanced on Araminta.

"You did come in handy," Olive continued. "My little tidbit about Angie and Owen sent you right to her and caused her to get rid of those letters."

"You knew about those too?" Araminta asked as she glanced around for a weapon.

"Of course. You were right about the apple not falling far from the tree. Shirley wasn't the only one that knew the family secrets. And since Angie knew her secret was out thanks to you, she decided to hide them in the dumbwaiter, which I'd conveniently reminded her of."

"You wanted her to toss them in the shaft." Araminta spied an old coal shovel to her left. If she could just distract Angie, she could grab it and have a fighting chance.

"That's right. Now I can prove to the police that *she* is the killer. It's too bad you were going to tell the police about her little affair and she had to kill you too. Luckily those letters will prove that she had the perfect motive."

Olive glanced toward the letters that had spilled out of the dumbwaiter, and Araminta saw her opportunity. She lurched sideways, grabbing the shovel and swinging it high over her head. To her dismay, the metal blade flew off, leaving her with a useless wooden handle.

Olive lunged forward!

Araminta held her palms up to ward off the attack. She squeezed her eyes shut, waiting for the painful stabs, but there was no pain. Instead, she heard a loud "oomph."

She opened her eyes to see Olive crumple to the floor.

Behind her, Daisy stood holding a plank of wood, her eyes wide as she stared down at Olive's still form.

"Daisy! Thank goodness you're here!" Araminta breathed in quickly then exhaled with relief. "How did you know where to find me?"

"Prudence. She said you were down here looking for mice, and I knew that couldn't be true. I guessed you might be on to something with the investigation. I sent Harold to the solarium to bring the police. They should be right behind me."

Araminta blew out her breath, relieved someone had come in time to save her. "Olive killed Shirley. She admitted everything."

Daisy nodded. "I heard. It's sad she tried to frame Angela."

Angela. Araminta hurried around Olive's prostrate body. The cats were one step ahead of her and already circling around the letters and batting them with their little paws. "Help me gather the letters, Daisy. Unless you'd like to deal with more family fallout, we will need to dispose of them."

Daisy hurriedly collected the papers, which had come out of the dumbwaiter opening when the thing fell. "Right. I don't think it's necessary for everyone to know about Angie and Owen's affair."

Quickly, she opened her purse and stuck them inside, along with the stack Araminta brought to her. She'd just managed to close the thing when the police came rushing down the stairs, with Harold right behind them.

CHAPTER TWENTY

"This flower arrangement is particularly colorful," Daisy said as she fussed with the purple and pink lilies, carnations, and chrysanthemums in the cut-crystal vase that sat on the sideboard in the parlor. Arun and Sasha must have agreed, because they immediately jumped up on to the sideboard and started sniffing.

"I'm just glad the relatives are gone." Reggie plopped down into an overstuffed chair, placing the duffel bag in front of him. He was on his way to make good on his promise of attending the Gamblers Anonymous retreat that afternoon.

"And that the real killer was caught and no one in our little family suffered." Araminta kept her eye on the cats. Lilies were poisonous for them, and she wanted to make sure they stuck to just sniffing and didn't try chewing. Though she knew they were smart and knew which plants to steer clear of, she didn't want to take any chances.

"Thanks to you." Stephanie squeezed Araminta's hand.

Araminta waved away the accolades. "All in a day's work."

"I think things turned out as good as can be expected." Daisy finished with the flowers and perched on the edge of the couch. "Even Prudence apologized for thinking there were mice in the manor."

Araminta smiled at the memory of Pru's apology. She'd even gone one step better and indicated that she should have known that such a problem would never have escaped Daisy's notice, given her attention to detail.

"It was a good thing she did hear those noises, though. Otherwise, I might not have figured out that the dumbwaiter was used for the murder weapon, and Olive may never have been caught, so some good came out of it, at least," Araminta said.

Another good thing had come of it, though Araminta couldn't tell the rest of the family. Only she and Daisy knew about the private moment with Angela, during which Daisy gave her the recovered letters with a stern reprimand about the absolute need for discretion if she meant to carry on with her extramarital frivolities. Daisy told Angela that she wouldn't take kindly to further blackening of the family reputation—especially after she and Araminta had done her a great favor by protecting her when they could have simply let the cops find her letters, which were open declarations of Angela's love and proof of her subsequent indiscretions with Daisy's own husband's brother.

No, the Moorecliff family had been through enough, and Daisy wouldn't appreciate further tarnishing of the Moorecliff name. Not at all.

Angela assured them both that her "fling" with Owen was over. She'd learned there was something to be said for loyalty within a family. She was going home to her husband, and who knew? Perhaps if she put a bit of actual effort into getting to know him, there might be a chance she would find more to love about her husband than the Moorecliff money.

Araminta was surprised by her declaration and skeptical about her sincerity, but Daisy felt assured Angela had taken Daisy's threat to heart and meant to change her ways. If there was one thing Araminta felt sure of, it was that Daisy often knew a lot more about people than they thought, so if she believed Angela was on the path to recovering a marriage she could have lost, well, she might as well believe it too.

"Poor Yancy, though," Stephanie said. "He's really down in the dumps."

All heads turned to look out the window, where Yancy was pruning a shrub. "Poor thing," Araminta said. "I think he'll be fine, though. I saw him exchanging information with Charlotte Dinsmore as she was leaving."

"Whatever makes him feel better, I guess. I do value the staff, and I want them to be happy." Daisy turned to Harold. "And I want to thank you for your part in helping the police take Olive into custody."

Olive had awakened when the police arrived after Daisy clobbered her and did not accept her arrest easily. Luckily, Harold was there to help Ivan and his uniformed officers wrangle her into the police car.

Harold blushed at the compliment. "A butler's job is to help in any way he can. I'm just glad that the killer was caught. Two murders at the manor in a matter of weeks is a bit unsettling."

Daisy laughed. "I'll say. We certainly have had our share of murders, but thankfully, that's behind us. With two under our belt, what are the odds murder will happen at Moorecliff Manor a third time?"

"Stay away from those lilies. They're toxic for cats," Sasha warned Arun, who was sniffing the colorful flower bouquet in the crystal vase.

Arun scowled. "I know that, silly. I was just trying to see if I could sniff out any intent."

"Intent?" Sasha glanced from Arun to the flowers.

"Yes, these flower deliveries keep coming for Daisy, but there is never any card. Who is sending them, and what is their intent?"

"A secret admirer, maybe?" Sasha suggested.

Arun shrugged and hopped down from the sideboard. "Wouldn't be the strangest thing going on around here."

"No kidding. Lots of strangeness with that Moorecliff clan. I'm just glad they are all gone."

"Ditto. They were disturbing my naps."

"And always trying to pick us up. I don't mind sometimes, but it was excessive."

Arun agreed. He much preferred to seek out attention rather than have it foisted on him. He didn't mind when Araminta or one of the immediate family scooped him up, but the attentions of the rest of the clan with their grabby hands were not welcome. He'd let them know that in no uncertain terms by hissing and clawing. "I especially did not relish the attention from Prudence after the old bag accused us of being inferior mousers!"

Sasha hissed her agreement. "Imagine her thinking there were mice on the premises. We would not allow it."

"No, the house is clean of intruders," Arun glanced out the window. "But maybe not the grounds."

Sasha followed his gaze. "So, you've notice too?"

Arun nodded. "Hedges trampled, footprints in the mulch, strange lingering smells."

"At first, I thought it was simply the nocturnal ramblings of the Moorecliff humans."

"But now that they are all gone…" Arun let his words drift off as they both stared out the window.

"We will have to keep an eye on the grounds. It's probably nothing." Sasha jumped down from the table, yawned, and stretched. "Right now, I think it's time to find a nice quiet place and catch up on my sleep."

"Good idea." Arun jumped down beside her. "You're right—it is probably nothing. Like Daisy said, what are the odds murder will happen at Moorecliff Manor a third time?"

****

Want more of the Moorecliff Manor series? Don't forget to grab the next book, Homicide in the Hydrangeas!

Sign up for my newsletter and I'll send you a link for a free download of a book in one of my other series:

https://leighanndobbscozymysteries.gr8.com

Join my readers group on Facebook:
https://www.facebook.com/groups/ldobbsreaders

Like my Facebook Author Page:
https://www.facebook.com/leighanndobbsbooks

Probable Paws

A Whisker of a Doubt

Wrong Side of the Claw

Claw and Order

Juniper Holiday Cozy Mysteries

***

Halloween Party Murder

Thanksgiving Dinner Death

Who Slayed The Santas?

Masquerade Party Murder

My Fatal Valentine

Oyster Cove Guesthouse

Cat Cozy Mystery Series

***

A Twist in the Tail

A Whisker in the Dark

A Purrfect Alibi

Kate Diamond Mystery Adventures

***

Hidden Agemda (Book 1)

Ancient Hiss Story (Book 2)

Heist Society (Book 3)

Silver Hollow

Paranormal Cozy Mystery Series

***

A Spell of Trouble (Book 1)

Spell Disaster (Book 2)

Nothing to Croak About (Book 3)

Cry Wolf (Book 4)

Shear Magic (Book 5)

Mooseamuck Island

Cozy Mystery Series

* * *

A Zen For Murder

A Crabby Killer

A Treacherous Treasure

Blackmoore Sisters

Cozy Mystery Series

* * *

Dead Wrong

Dead & Buried

Dead Tide

Buried Secrets

Deadly Intentions

A Grave Mistake

Spell Found

Fatal Fortune

Hidden Secrets

Lexy Baker

Cozy Mystery Series

* * *

Killer Cupcakes

Dying For Danish

Murder, Money and Marzipan

3 Bodies and a Biscotti

Brownies, Bodies & Bad Guys

Bake, Battle & Roll

Wedded Blintz

Scones, Skulls & Scams

Ice Cream Murder

Mummified Meringues

Brutal Brulee (Novella)

No Scone Unturned

Cream Puff Killer

Never Say Pie

Ain't Seen Muffin Yet

Assault and Buttercream

Lady Katherine Regency Mysteries

***

An Invitation to Murder (Book 1)

The Baffling Burglaries of Bath (Book 2)

Murder at the Ice Ball (Book 3)

A Murderous Affair (Book 4)

Murder on Charles Street (Book 5)

Julia and Nora Marsh 1920s Cozy Mystery

***

Murder on a Mississippi Steamboat

Hazel Martin Historical Mystery Series

***

Murder at Lowry House (book 1)

Murder by Misunderstanding (book 2)

Sam Mason Mysteries
(As L. A. Dobbs)

***

Telling Lies (Book 1)

Keeping Secrets (Book 2)

Exposing Truths (Book 3)

Betraying Trust (Book 4)

Killing Dreams (Book 5)

More books in the Rockford Security Series:

Cold As Her Heart

A Game of Kill

No One To Trust

No Time To Run

Don't Fear The Truth

Hide From The Past

Romantic Comedy

****

Corporate Chaos Series

In Over Her Head (book 1)

Can't Stand the Heat (book 2)

What Goes Around Comes Around (book 3)

Careful What You Wish For (4)

Dish Best Served Cold (5)

Contemporary Romance

***

Reluctant Romance

Sweet Romance (Written As Annie Dobbs)

Firefly Inn Series

***

Another Chance (Book 1)

Another Wish (Book 2)

Hometown Hearts Series

***

No Getting Over You (Book 1)

A Change of Heart (Book 2)

Sweet Mountain Billionaires

***

Jaded Billionaire (Book 1)

A Billion Reasons Not To Fall In Love (Book 2)

***

Sweetrock Sweet and Spicy Cowboy Romance

Some Like It Hot

Too Close For Comfort

———

Regency Romance

* * *

Scandals and Spies Series:

Kissing The Enemy

Deceiving the Duke

Tempting the Rival

Charming the Spy

Pursuing the Traitor

Captivating the Captain

The Unexpected Series:

An Unexpected Proposal

An Unexpected Passion

Dobbs Fancytales:

Dobbs Fancytales Boxed Set Collection

———

Western Historical Romance

***

Goldwater Creek Mail Order Brides:

Faith

American Mail Order Brides Series:

Chevonne: Bride of Oklahoma

Magical Romance with a Touch of Mystery

***

Something Magical

Curiously Enchanted

ABOUT THE AUTHOR

USA Today best-selling Author, Leighann Dobbs, has had a passion for reading since she was old enough to hold a book, but she didn't put pen to paper until much later in life. After a twenty-year career as a software engineer, with a few side trips into selling antiques and making jewelry, she realized you can't make a living reading books, so she tried her hand at writing them and discovered she had a passion for that, too! She lives in New Hampshire with her husband, Bruce, their trusty Chihuahua mix, Mojo, and beautiful rescue cat, Kitty.

Find out about her latest books by signing up at:
https://leighanndobbscozymysteries.gr8.com

If you want to receive a text message alert on your cell phone for new releases , text COZYMYSTERY to 88202 (sorry, this only works for US cell phones!)

Connect with Leighann on Facebook
http://facebook.com/leighanndobbsbooks

This is a work of fiction.

None of it is real. All names, places, and events are products of the author's imagination. Any resemblance to real names, places, or events are purely coincidental, and should not be construed as being real.

STABBED IN THE SOLARIUM

Copyright © 2021

Leighann Dobbs Publishing

http://www.leighanndobbs.com

All Rights Reserved.

No part of this work may be used or reproduced in any manner, except as allowable under "fair use," without the express written permission of the author.

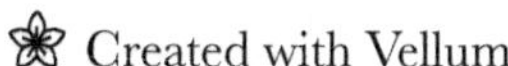 Created with Vellum